T0064580

Evil By Nature

HUNTER KARR

BALBOA.
PRESS
A DIVISION OF HAY HOUSE

Balboa Press books may be ordered through booksellers or by contacting:

Balboa Press
A Division of Hay House
1663 Liberty Drive
Bloomington, IN 47403
www.balboapress.com
1 (877) 407-4847

Because of the dynamic nature of the Internet, any web addresses or links contained in this book may have changed since publication and may no longer be valid. The views expressed in this work are solely those of the author and do not necessarily reflect the views of the publisher, and the publisher hereby disclaims any responsibility for them.

The author of this book does not dispense medical advice or prescribe the use of any technique as a form of treatment for physical, emotional, or medical problems without the advice of a physician, either directly or indirectly. The intent of the author is only to offer information of a general nature to help you in your quest for emotional and spiritual well-being. In the event you use any of the information in this book for yourself, which is your constitutional right, the author and the publisher assume no responsibility for your actions.

Any people depicted in stock imagery provided by Thinkstock are models, and such images are being used for illustrative purposes only.
Certain stock imagery © Thinkstock.

Print information available on the last page.

ISBN: 978-1-5043-3583-6 (sc)
ISBN: 978-1-5043-3585-0 (hc)
ISBN: 978-1-5043-3584-3 (e)

Library of Congress Control Number: 2015910368

Balboa Press rev. date: 07/08/2015

Dedications

This book has been a long time coming. There have been many stumbles along the way but somehow it got finished. There are many people I would like to dedicate this book to that I don't know where to start. If I have forgotten anybody, I truly apologize.

First and foremost I would like to thank my family, especially my grandfather, God rest his soul. He was always there for me no matter what and he always made me feel as if I could do anything. You are the reason I am here today. I miss you grandpa. My beautiful daughters, we all have had our ups and downs but I will always love you. You are the other reason for my existence and the reason I have so many beautiful grand children today.

Tara Yeager, what can I say about you (that would be safe to say out loud)? You're the best friend a person could have asked for. Most of the ideas have come from your head (which is scary but……..) needless to say, without your input and friendship I don't think I would have made it as far as I have, thank you.

Brandy McCleary, you definitely are one of a kind. We have been through a lot, and that has helped shape my thinking of this whole venture. I don't know what I would do without you. And I promise, I will keep your husband alive (thank God *you* know what I am talking about).

Sergeant Rodney Fontaine, you're a great man who has helped me more than you know. Thank you, you're my hero (rather you want to hear it or not). And many thanks for all of your technical help with the writing of this book. Your input has been more valuable than you realize.

And many thanks to so many more out there. I hope that I will be able to continue my writing, it is such good therapy. I also hope I get to keep in contact with my many characters, they definitely are an interesting bunch!

Chapter 1

"Do you know how much that shit cost?" Robert yelled.

"It's not like you paid for it, mom did! Like everything else, mom paid for it because SHE is the only one working!" Cassie exclaimed. "Do you even know what it's like to work? Have *you* ever worked a day in your life?"

"You ungrateful little bitch! If you were my daughter you would never have gotten away with talking to me like that or I would have beaten your ass." Robert screamed.

"I would have killed myself if I were your daughter. My mother never should have married you. I tried to tell her what kind of a fucking snake you are but she wouldn't listen. One of these days she will see the truth about you. Mom will know that you are nothing but a lazy, good for nothing; pervert and I will make sure that I see you in hell!" Cassie screamed back.

Before she knew it her left cheek was bright red and it stung. It took a couple of seconds for her to realize that Robert had slapped her.

"You're going to pay for that! I'm going to tell mom that you have been abusing me. Then she will leave you and your ass will be living in a fucking cardboard box like you deserve!" Cassie screamed.

Just then Robert wrapped his long, bony fingers around her throat and jacked her up against the side of the trailer. Cassie's long, thick, red hair was twisted around his fingers and she was straining to move her head. "What…do…you…think…you're…doing?" Cassie mustered to spit out.

"Like I said, you *will* respect me"

"Fuck you. Let go of me!"

"The fuck I will. You ever talk to me like that again and your mother will never believe you ever. I will make sure that she knows that you are nothing but a lying, whoring, little bitch and when I am done, she will believe me or she will be taught a rough lesson, the hard way!" Robert spit out.

Just as he was about to loosen his fingers just a little, Cassie's right knee folded up and thrust forward, hard. Robert crumpled instantly. Cassie ran. But as she started to run away, she yelled one last comment. "You ever touch me or my mother again; I will see you dead!"

"What are we going to do boss?" Shorty asked.

"Don't you worry about it. I know who is going to take care of that sonovabitch! He will pay for what he did to my family. Now go find Frankie and tell him that I want to talk to him." Anthony ordered.

With that order, Shorty left. Anthony, pacing about the floor in his office, never thought that his only daughter would have been raped. 'Who the hell would be stupid enough to cross me like that?' he thought. Finally sitting down behind his desk, Anthony began thinking. Picking up the phone, he spoke into the receiver and said five words that would change everybody's lives in a little town in Michigan forever.

North Muskegon is a little town just east of Lake Michigan. With a population of just over four thousand year round residents, it contains a few banks, a fire station, police station, state park, a few restaurants, its share of grocery stores and gas stations. There are two schools that take pride in their academics and have some of the best athletes that could compete with the best of the best.

North Muskegon has never seen anything horrific in its almost 125 year history. But its citizens would soon see what it's like to be afraid. For its residents and business owners alike, along with the police, will find a reign of terror that it has never seen before.

"Cassie, what the hell is the matter with you? What happened to your face?" Brandie asked.

"Nothing, I just hate my mother's husband. She can't see that he isn't the perfect man that she married. My grandpa tried to tell her not to marry him. Hell, even my uncles tried to tell her but no, mom wouldn't hear any of it. All she could think of is getting someone to take care of her so she wouldn't have to work and could sit on her ass all day long. Brandie, she won't listen to me." Cassie exclaimed.

"She won't listen to what? What have you tried to tell her?"

"Never mind. Don't worry about it. I am just pissed off and rambling." Cassie said. She couldn't get up the courage to tell her best friend what had really happened. She couldn't bear the thought of Brandie knowing what was going on at home. For if she did, she could lose the only friend she had ever known. Cassie might have lost a lot in her life, but she wasn't about to lose the one person who she trusted.

"Cassie. Are you ok?"

"Yeah I am fine. Now what do you have that we can eat? I am starving."

"Hey Cass. How did that job interview go? Did you get the job at that coffee shop?"

"The interview went great. Or at least I thought it did. When I was there it was really busy and I had to wait a few minutes for my interview but I really hope I get the job. That would get me out of the house and I can start saving up money so I can get the hell out of here! I want to go back to Chicago where I belong."

"Well when that time comes, I'm going with you." Brandie stated.

"You do know that it's going to be a long time before I leave, right?"

"Yeah I know. But until then we need to have fun while we are waiting."

"Brandie, where are your mom and dad? Shouldn't they be here by now? I mean it's already 5pm."

"Mom had to stop at the grocery store and get stuff for dinner and dad is working late at the pharmacy. Mom said that she would be home by 5:30pm and yes I already told her that you were staying the night, so don't worry."

"Look, Brandie, I don't want to get you into any trouble. I know that you just moved in and that you all have things to do. I can go home. I will just see you at school tomorrow. I just needed to talk to someone."

"Don't even think about it. Mom likes you and she knows that Robert isn't the best person in the world. I wouldn't feel right knowing that you were home alone with him anyway. He gives me the creeps. There is just something about him that makes me feel like I have seen him somewhere before, like I know him from somewhere. I don't know I can't place it. Something isn't right with him. So don't even think about leaving. Plus you need to help me get my room cleaned so I can set up for my new water bed."

"Fine. But one thing first, would you go with me to get my stuff? I have to get my backpack and some clothes." Cassie said.

"Damn. And to think that my mom locked up her gun!"

"See, not funny. He isn't worth it anyway. But I will say that when he does die, I will dance on his grave."

"Talking about moms, where is Mrs. Yeager?" Brandie asked.

"No telling. Probably at the store buying a bunch of shit, considering she got her food stamps today."

"Well at least you will have food for a little while."

"Yeah, whatever. Let's go and get this done and over with before I change my mind."

The Johnson household was one you thought you would only see in the movies; a father that worked hard for his family; a mother that loved her job, her husband and an their only daughter. And a daughter that knew what it was like to help people.

Mr. and Mrs. Johnson did a good job in raising their daughter. They knew that one day Brandie was going to do great things. But what they didn't know was that their little girl was going to turn over a hornet's nest, the likes of nothing they ever knew before. And when it was over, their family would be intertwined forever.

Fall was a great time. Not too hot, not too cool, just right. Michigan has one of the greatest fall color tours ever to be found. A long look around town would leave you awestruck.

The trees are the perfect colors of gold, red and yellow. The leaves are just starting to turn and football season is in full swing. And the mild winds that come off Muskegon Lake make you want to thank Mother Nature for the beauty her handiwork provides.

When the girls arrived, they found Robert passed out on the couch. The miserable drunk that he was, never missed a chance to drink. Hell he would get on his peddle bike and ride the edge of the freeways collecting bottles and cans just so he could have money to drink. Never mind that he supposedly had a family to take care of and that he should have been working. No, he would rather be drinking and making sexual advances at his wife's daughter.

Warily, they quietly walked into the trailer and went straight to Cassie's room. *So far so good,* she thought as she began putting clothes in another backpack. *God please don't let him wake up.* "Brandie, grab my bag and let's get the hell out of here!" she whispered.

Cassie hated Robert, but Brandie hated him more. She knew that he was the reason all the neighborhood children didn't go anywhere without their parents. She also knew that someday Robert would pay for what he was doing to her best friend and so many other people around her that she cared about.

Chapter 2

It was a long time before Cassie could fall asleep. It wasn't the fact that she was not sleeping in her own bed, it was because she still didn't feel safe. She knew that Brandie's parents had a security system installed when they first moved in but something still bothered her about everything.

It was pitch black in Brandie's room since she couldn't sleep with any lights or noises, so all Cassie could do was let her mind wander a little too much. She thought about earlier in the day when she got into that argument with Robert and he attacked her. She thought about the dream she had two nights ago. She just couldn't go to sleep to save her ass.

Just as she thought she was dozing off, Cassie heard glass breaking in the kitchen. She tried to wake Brandie but she wouldn't wake up. All Brandie did was moan a little and turn over. *Damn it why isn't anybody waking up, why isn't the alarm going off?* Cassie thought.

Against her better judgment, Cassie got up to see what was happening. Slowly she walked down the hall towards Jamie and Terri's room at the other end of the house. Once she approached the kitchen Cassie looked and to her surprise, she didn't notice anything. No broken windows, nothing amiss, there was nothing out of place.

Cassie began yelling down the hall towards Brandie's parents' room, but nothing. The closer she looked, the darker it got. It wasn't until she reached their door that she thought she heard a voice. For a second

Cassie felt relief. She thought to herself, it must have been a dream and decided to walk back to Brandie's room.

When she approached the kitchen again, Cassie stepped on shards of broken glass, cutting the bottom of her right foot. *Sonovabitch,* she cursed to herself. Then in a flash, somebody hit her on the back of the head, knocking her out.

You little bitch; I told you if you ever fucking crossed me again that you would pay. But you didn't listen. I told you that you're no good mother is going to see you in hell. I also told you that she wouldn't believe anything you told her. Did you really think that you were going to be able to go about life without me?

Look at me! I didn't give you permission to move, you ungrateful little whore. What do you think your mom said when I told her that you came on to me?

Cassie couldn't talk; her mouth was duct taped shut. She could barely see out of her right eye. The beating was enough to make her wish that she was already dead. The pain she felt in both of her shoulders felt like somebody had jammed railroad stakes through both of them.

Hanging there under a support beam, her wrists bound together by handcuffs, Cassie knew she was going to die.

She knew that something wasn't right when she heard that noise. She knew that Robert was going to come and get her. But the thing that she didn't understand was why Brandie and her parents didn't hear when she yelled. Why did they ignore her? Why didn't they stop him?

Hey. Hey, pay attention! I told you that nobody was going to believe you and there isn't a damn thing you can do to save yourself. I told you that you were mine, and only mine. I will do what I please with you and nobody can stop me.

Without warning, Robert thrust a red hot poker right into Cassie's abdomen. The pain was so severe that she couldn't get any sounds out. The smell was so awful that bile rushed up to the back of her throat.

"That felt good didn't it? He asked her. I know all about you, you like pain. I know how you look at me when you get home from school, how you want me to hurt you. Well you're getting it all now." Then with one more bit of strength, Cassie opened her good eye. That's when she seen it, the glimmer of her kitchen knife. Right as Robert placed the tip of the knife to her throat

and began to slice, Cassie gathered the last bit of strength she had and screamed and this time..........

"Cassie, Cassie! Wake up! It's only a dream! Mom, help me she won't wake up!" Brandie screamed.

Rushing into Brandie's room, Terri stood there with Brandie while Jamie gently shook Cassie trying to wake her. "Cassie honey wake up, you're having a bad dream."

Cassie shot up straight up in bed like it was on fire. Still panicking, she screamed "He's trying to kill me and you guys won't stop him!"

"Cassie, honey you were having a bad dream. You are ok, you're safe here. Nobody was trying to kill you."

Finally starting to calm, Cassie told Jamie "Mrs. Johnson, don't you get it? He was trying to kill me. Robert was here. He broke into your house; he broke a window and came in here." She said as she broke down into tears and began shaking.

Jamie sat down on to the edge of the bed and cradled Cassie, while looking at Terri and Brandie. "Shhh. It will be ok. I promise you nobody came in here and tried to hurt you. All the windows are perfectly fine. Why don't you lie back down and try to get some rest. We will leave a light on if it will make you feel better."

After a few minutes, Cassie conceded and lay back down. Jamie turned on Brandie's bedside lamp as her and Terri walked out of the bedroom. They both had a look of concern on their faces as they walked towards their bedroom. "Terri, what happened to that poor child? What could that sonovabitch have done to her to make that happen?"

"I don't know honey. I know it can't be easy for her living there with him. Just watching him makes me want to choke him myself. I do know that we better make sure that that bastard doesn't go anywhere near our daughter."

"Terri, something isn't right. They always say that nightmares stem from a level of truth. She will never tell us what's going on but we should let her stay here as much as possible, for as long as we can. Maybe that way she can get a sense of safety. I'm not saying that Jessica knows what's going on or anything but damn, if it was my daughter I would hope that somebody would want to help her."

"Of course, she can stay as long as possible. But if her mom or step father says no, there will be nothing that we can do about it."

"I know. But we have to try to do something. What kind of people would we be if we just turned a blind eye and did nothing? Terri, promise me one thing. That Robert doesn't hurt another soul?"

"We will do what we can, I promise."

Jamie and Terri returned back to their bedroom and turned their lights off. But Jamie had a sense of dread come over her, because somehow she knew what he was doing to her. Somehow she knew him. Turning off the lamp, she knew that Robert was doing something to Cassie, and she wondered how bad it was. For if it came right down to it, she thought to herself that she would make sure that he would be stopped by whatever means possible.

"Brandie, I'm sorry for you having to have to see that. I am sorry that I didn't just stay home. I never should have put you through that. I didn't mean to wake you by my nightmare."

"Cassie, stop it. You have no control over your dreams; you do not have to apologize for it. You can stay here as long as you want. I know my mom and dad aren't going to care. Especially after what they just seen you go through. Now go ahead and lie down and try to get some sleep ok?"

Reluctantly, Cassie took her friends advice and put her head back down on the pillow. Not knowing what was fantasy or what was reality anymore, she closed her eyes and prayed. She prayed for some peace even if it was only for the night. Cassie was afraid of not knowing the difference anymore. She didn't know what to do or if anything could be done.

Brandie thought to herself, with her eyes closed, that Robert has hurt her for the last time. She knew that if she didn't do something she would regret it. Cassie was her one true friend and if she didn't do something now, she would never forgive herself.

Before Brandie drifted off to sleep, she had a thought; of how Robert would be stopped. Would the police listen to a teenager? How could she get them to listen to her? They needed to know just what kind of monster lived in their town. Robert Yeager was a bad man. He was evil by nature.

Chapter 3

Cassie quietly walked into her trailer, after leaving Brandie's house early the next morning, hoping and praying that nobody was home. She looked both ways and listened for anything. *Maybe nobody is here, she thought.*

"Cassie, honey, I need you to sit down. We need to talk before Robert comes back home from wherever he is at." Jessica said as she walked out of her bedroom.

"Mom, what do you want? I have things to do". *Damn it.*

"Just please, sit down and when I'm done you can leave if you want." Jessica said.

"Fine, whatever, can we just hurry?"

"Look what I am about to tell you is not going to be easy to say for me or easy for you to hear. You just need to know that no matter what, I love you without hesitation. You are the best thing that ever happened to me. You need to understand that."

"Mom, what's wrong? Are you sick? You're not going to die on me are you?"

"No honey. I'm not sick. Although having to relive this hell is sickening enough. Wow, ok. 18 years ago I was raped, when I lived in New Jersey. I was walking home from work, it was late, hell it was dark. He must have been following me for a long time, because I didn't know anybody was behind me. I was unlocking my door to my apartment and the next thing I knew, I was being forced into the apartment by someone wearing a mask. He forced my clothes off, threw me on the bed..." Jessica now tears flowing down her face, couldn't make herself finish the sentence. Even she didn't know if she could finish because of having to relive that horrendous night or if she didn't want Cassie to have to go through it with her.

Fear breached Cassie's face. Eyes wide open, not knowing if she could trust herself to speak; all she could do was cry. Every ounce of strength that Cassie had washed away when her mother was done telling her that she thought that she was the product of rape.

"Mom, I don't know what to say. Are you...ok?"

"I'm sorry honey I just thought that it was for the best. Not telling you until you were ready. It was some time later, after I moved that I found out that you weren't the product of rape; I was already pregnant when it happened. I have made such a mess of my life, could you ever forgive me? I have always done what I thought was best for you."

"Mom, do you know who my real father is? I mean I think after hearing all of this I can handle hearing about who my real father is. Does he know that I exist? Did he know you were pregnant? Why did he leave you pregnant like that? I mean that is so wrong!"

"Cassie, calm down. No he didn't know I was pregnant. Hell I didn't know that I was pregnant already until after I left town. No he doesn't know about you. I don't know where he lives or if he is married. I do know that he was a strong and beautiful man. He is probably already married and has kids of his own. I mean that was 18 years ago. I don't even know how to go about trying to find him. I left him with a note because I was too ashamed to tell him what happened. He didn't deserve the headache. He deserved better than me. He probably hates me."

"Mom, we will get through it. If you want help, all you have to do is ask. You don't know if my father is married or not. He might not be..."

"Cassie. We are talking about New Jersey honey. That was a long time ago in a different state. There is no way that we can find him, even if I wanted to. Besides I am married now and I will not step outside my vows."

"Those vows aren't shit mom, Robert isn't a good person and you know it. You told me the truth, so now it's my turn. I have to tell you something. I know you want to believe that he is a good guy but Robert is not the person you should have wanted to marry. He is a mistake. I can't place it but there is something not right with him. I can't..."

"Look, I know you don't like him but…"

"Mom! Damn it! He tried to rape me. He had me in choke hold up against the trailer. The only reason I didn't tell you was because he threatened to kill you if I did. Did you know that the FBI is here? In this town! I know they are here because of him. Why else would the feds be in a town like this. Everything was ok until he showed up." Cassie said as she stormed out.

Jessica was up against the proverbial brick wall. Knowing what happened to her years ago and then having to deal with the possibility of her husband touching her daughter? *He wouldn't do that, he's a drunk, not a monster.* Jessica thought to herself. But did she believe it? Sagging down in the old broken down couch, she sighed to herself. *Why? Could it be possible? Robert wouldn't do that. But why **IS** the FBI in town?*

Looking out the window, on to the road Jessica wondered what the truth was anymore. She wondered what happened to Chewy. She loved him so much; it killed her to leave him. Jessica started to cry as she thought about that fateful night, the night she turned her back on the one person who almost saved her. She fought so hard with her mom over him

"Chewy is a good man mom. He is strong; he believes in family, how can you not like him?"

"He's Mexican Jessica. How can you not see my point? Do you really think that your dad will be ok with it? I am sure that he is a good man. And even I know that not every Mexican is bad but you have to see it from my point. What do you think your father will say?"

"I don't care what daddy will say about it. I love him and I don't care what nationality he is. He wants to marry me. He loves me for me and that's all that matters."

"Jessica, why don't you just think about it a while and then I am sure that you will come up with a fresh frame of mind."

"I'm not changing my mind mother, no matter how long I sleep on it."

"Jessica, you will regret it later if you stay with him."

"How mother? Huh? How the hell do you figure? It is my life nobody else's. If we don't care about mixed relationships why the hell should anybody else? It's nobody else's business but ours."

"Jessica, you know what will happen if you continue to see him. Your father will disown you." "And because you are too scared to stand up to daddy, you wouldn't even stand up for your own daughter? Why the hell did you even have me then anyway? You know what? Don't bother to answer that. It won't matter anyway. You're a coward and daddy is a bully. What a perfect fucking family!"

Jessica rubbed the side of her cheek. It was almost as if that slap was just yesterday.

"I'm sorry honey; you just make me so mad sometimes."

"Why does that not surprise me? You hit your own daughter but you can't even look your own abusive husband in the eye! We are done here mother. I am old enough to make my own decisions. You will not make them for me. Good luck living with daddy. Bye mother."

With that being said, Jessica walked out of her parent's life once and for all. The next thing she knew, someone told her that her mother was dead. She was sad, but not surprised. Her daddy was abusive, and that was one reason why Jessica had to leave.

It was just an added perk that she met Chewy when she did.

Chewy was something. Six foot 4', 230 pounds, black hair and not an ounce of fat on him. Jessica knew that he wouldn't even look her way. Why would someone like him want anything to do with her? So she moved on, kept shopping. The next thing she knew, he was behind her in the checkout lane. They made small talk, while they were waiting and the next thing she knew, Jessica had given Chewy her phone number.

Jessica knew better than to wait by the phone, or so she thought. Chewy kept her on the phone for hours talking about nothing but everything. She found out that both of them loved sports, animals and classical music. They both hate racism and neither cared what other people thought of interracial relationships.

It was that night that Jessica knew she had met her destiny. She didn't care if people would think that she was too young. She loved Chewy and that's all that mattered. They were together for six months before she told her mother about Chewy. And at the end of that night, Jessica walked out of her parent's house for good.

Life was good with Chewy. He never raised a hand to Jessica. They both finished high school. They were careful with sex and worked hard to keep that little apartment they shared in Hackensack, NJ.

Chewy worked twelve hour shifts at the landfill in Lyndhurst. And when he wasn't working, he was going to school to major in Criminal Justice. Jessica worked as a bartender in Hackensack five days a week. She didn't get to spend much time with Chewy, but the time they did get to have together, was priceless. He would prepare candlelit dinners for them, and they would cuddle for hours.

But then one night while Chewy was working late, Jessica was attacked as she entered her apartment. She never called the police, never looked back. She left him that night with just a note that said she had to leave. No explanation, just a note telling him that she loved him with all of her heart and hopefully one day he would forgive her.

Jessica was still thinking about what she had said to her daughter and what her daughter had told her. Could it be real? She didn't want to face the possibility that her husband was a monster. *Should I go to the police and find out what is really going on?* Jessica thought to herself. What could be the harm in talking to someone? With that thought, Jessica dried her face, put on a little makeup to hide the tear streaks and walked out the door.

Driving to the police station, Jessica kept thinking about Chewy and what she had done to him, about her daughter and what she had said and Robert's mannerisms the past few months. *He had been acting a little odd but not bad enough to touch Cassie.* Pulling into a parking spot at the police station, she couldn't help but think about their conversation, wondering if any of it could be true.

Sensory overload to its highest. All Jessica could do was stand there and look and listen. It seemed like hundreds of phones were ringing and people were everywhere. People handcuffed to chairs, policemen walking in with people handcuffed. People bitching "I'm telling you, I didn't do it. Are you fucking listening to me?" One woman said.

Ringing the bell to get some attention, Jessica wanted to talk to someone before she lost her nerve and walk out. The desk sergeant finally turned around, "May I help you?"

"Is the Sheriff in? I need to talk to him."

"What's your name ma'am?" Sergeant said.

"Mmy..name..? Mmyy..name is Jessica Yeager."

"Are you ok ma'am? You look a little under the weather. Can I get you some water while you are waiting for Sheriff Garcia?"

"I'm fine, but water would be good, thanks."

Jessica sat down where the desk sergeant indicated and then he brought her some water. There was just something about this station that creeped her out. Jessica just watched two men in black suits walk by her and up to the desk. Then they were off again, when they were shuffled into a windowless room.

Jessica was watching the two suited men when someone to her left said something. She turned her head and there stood a very tall, good looking man. Sheriff Garcia was tall slightly overweight but the ladies still thought he was handsome. But Jessica wasn't even thinking about it because she was still upset about previous matters early in the day.

When Jessica stood, and made eye contact with the sheriff, he lost color and almost fell over. "Are you ok sheriff? You look a little pale."

"Sheriff. Are you ok?" the desk sergeant asked.

"Thank you, but I am ok. I believe I am just getting the flu. I understand that you want to talk to me. Anything specific?"

"Yes I would like to talk to you about my daughter and my husband."

"Ok follow me ma'am."

They walked into the sheriff's office and he shut the door. Sheriff Garcia went behind his desk and pointed to the chair across from him for Jessica to sit down.

"Please tell me, how can I help you? It's not too often that someone insists on talking to me. Usually, I let my men take care of such things. Why me?" He asked.

"I can't explain sir..." He waved a hand trying to stop her.

"Please call me Ray."

"Ok, Ray, but as I said I can't explain it but it seems like you are the only one that I feel I can trust. My daughter says that her stepfather attacked her yesterday. She says that the FBI are here in town and I don't know what to make of my husband. I mean my daughter and I had a talk to today and I have to agree with her. Something isn't right.

I don't know why I am telling you all of this or why I am really here but something's not right definitely.

"Let's start with you telling me your husband and daughter's name." Ray said.

"Well my husband's name is Robert Yeager and my daughters' name is Cassie Damian."

When Sheriff Garcia heard those two names, he lost all color again. He knew now why the feds were in the other room waiting for him. He knew what was going on. He knew who Robert and Cassie were and he knew when destiny came pounding on his door.

Chapter 4

"Baby, are you sure that you are going to be home by then?"

"Yes honey I'm sure. Now you have to let me go so I can get my work done."

With that quick conversation, Terri hung up. He had to make sure that he didn't mess up anybody's medications. Being a pharmacist was stressful. It had its long hours, not knowing when something could go wrong, having to deal with irate customers. Then there is having to be smart enough to know what you're doing when you have to mix meds.

Terri had his suspicions about Robert. He never trusted him, never liked him. He didn't like how Robert would watch Jamie and Brandie when they were outside. Terri always felt like Robert was a sicko and a pervert and whenever he would get the chance he would act on it. Terri never felt comfortable around him.

Terri tried to be personable to Robert, but there was just something about him that he couldn't trust. He couldn't put his finger on it, but something wasn't right. And then when he heard that the feds were in town, he knew that they were here because of Robert, he just didn't know why but he knew that it had to do with Robert.

Even though Brandie wasn't his real daughter, he always treated her like she was his own and the thought of some sick bastard laying his hands on her, made his stomach curl. Jamie was just one semester shy of graduation when she met Terri on campus.

Terri enrolled in classes to become a pharmacist and Jamie was studying to become a nurse. They hit it off instantly and spent every waking moment together. Theirs was a chemistry that could not be contained and before long they caught themselves finishing each other's sentences. Love was definitely there.

After about a year, Terri proposed to Jamie and with tears in her eyes, she said yes. Everything was going along perfectly until two weeks before their wedding, Jamie was walking home from class and before she knew it, a tall, scrawny built man in a ski mask came up from behind and dragged her into the alley and brutally beat and raped her.

Jamie didn't have the courage to tell Terri about the attack. She couldn't bear the thought of having to try and tell the man that she loved, that what should have been his was taken away from her. The shame of it all was almost too much for her, she contemplated suicide but had it not been for Terri and his undying love for her, she would have ended it right then and there. So all Jamie could do was go through with the wedding and pray that Terri wouldn't find out about it.

When Jamie found out that she was pregnant, she was terrified, and Terri was ecstatic. He loved the thought of being a father. He started buying baby clothes, and all of the essentials. And all the while Jamie kept praying and hoping that the baby was Terri's.

It wasn't until later when Brandie was born and needed a blood transfusion for a medical condition called Aplastic Anemia, which they found after the hospital ran routine tests. It was then that Jamie had no choice but to explain to Terri that she was raped and found out that she was pregnant and that Terri was not the father. Terri was angry, hurt and in shock of course but he knew that Brandie, an innocent child, was not at fault. Terri agreed that they were not to tell Brandie who she was and where she came from and that Terri would love her like she was his own child.

'Ok that's enough' Terri thought to himself. He knew that if he kept thinking back he would get more pissed off. Terri was there for Brandie's birth, her first steps, and even for her first date.

Never had he ever thought that he would have to deal with something that would hit so close to home. Terri went about his business, filling prescriptions and answering customers' questions but he couldn't help himself, his mind would still wonder from time to time.

Terri had his suspicions about who Robert was and why the FBI was here. He couldn't put his finger on it but, he knew it wasn't good. Terri checked his messages on his cell phone because he noticed the icon on the screen was present. As he listened a light bulb went off in his head *Shit, this can't be happening here. I knew he looked familiar* and realized something, he knew why the feds were in town. It didn't take rocket science to figure out why everybody was scrambling to either protect Robert or would at least want to talk to him.

Forcing it down, Terri focused on protecting his family, and those close to his family. He knew that Cassie was close to his daughter and that Cassie's mom Jessica was being backed into a metaphorical corner by Robert and that's why she hasn't left him yet. Terri also knew that Robert had to be stopped. He also knew that one way or another Terri would make sure that Robert Yeager could not hurt another loved one let alone any other human being again.

Chapter 5

"Mrs. Yeager, let me start off by saying that…"

"Sheriff, are you ok. You look a little peaked again. Hey do I know you? You look familiar. And please, call me Jessica."

If she only knew! How could she not know, how could she not remember? But I guess with a husband like Robert, I can see why. Ray thought. *But I'll be damned if anything will happen to them. So help me. Easy Ray, settle down. She has no clue.*

"I am fine. Look Jessica, there is no easy way to say this but I believe your daughter is in danger and telling the truth. Plus just a couple of days ago, we had an anonymous tip that put validity to your daughter's story. They say they seen your *husband* trying to choke Cassie. So I am sorry but it seems as if your daughter is right. It seems as if there is a lot that you don't know about your husband." Ray said as he choked the words out.

He was sweating now. Trying to keep his feelings and anger in check. Telling Jessica that her so called husband was a monster was like trying to patch a crack on the Hoover Dam with a band aid.

"Sheriff, what are you not telling me? I mean the minute I walked in you look like you have seen a ghost and now you are sweating so bad that you look like you could be a spokes model for Hydrosal Gel. Now talk Ray or I am leaving."

Wow some things never change. Ray said to himself with a smile on his face.

"Ok, Robert is not who you think he is. You said that Cassie swears that the FBI is here, well she is right. They are in the next room waiting for me. They want to talk to me about Robert.

But the minute that I tell them that you are here, they would have my ass for not letting them talk to you. I think that the safest thing to do is let them explain everything to you. Will you escort me to the next room?"

"Look Sheriff, I came to talk to you. Not somebody in a rent a suit and a bad toupee."

"Jessica I promise, I will be right there next to you. I will hold your hand if you want me to. But I think that it is for the best if we go in and talk to the FBI. It will probably be hard for you to hear most of it but I assure you, your husband is not a nice person."

"Fine, if I don't like what's going on, I will get up and walk out. And you will not stop me. I don't care if they are the FBI or not. I will not be threatened." With that being said, Jessica got up and followed Sheriff Garcia down the hall. Little did she know, that her life was about to be turned into a movie of the week.

"This is Jessica Yeager, the wife of the man of why you are here. Please have a seat." Ray said as he pointed to the chairs in front of him. Always the gentlemen, Ray pulled out a chair next to him for Jessica. *I am not letting her out of my sight this time.*

Sitting in the big conference room was kind of intimidating for Jessica. But somehow she felt safe knowing that Sheriff Garcia was sitting next to her. She felt like she knew him. But she couldn't place it. What was it? Maybe it would come to her later.

"My name is Special Agent Darryl Johnson and that's my partner Agent Andrew Donaldson. Thank you for agreeing to talk to us Mrs. Yeager. Let me start by telling you that you are not in any trouble. We just want to talk to you about your husband. Ok?" SA Johnson said.

"Fine. But let me tell you one thing, if I don't like how this is going, I can and will leave. Now what do you want?"

"You're right sheriff, she is a special one. Does she know?"

"No not yet. I figured you should be the one to tell her."

"What have you told her so far?"

"Not much other than her husband is not who she thinks he is." Ray was not about to tell them that about their conversation yet. He didn't trust people right off the bat, especially the feds.

"Helllooo...." Jessica said as she waved her hands in front of everybody. "Do I have to be here for this? You do know that I am right here and the last time I had my hearing checked it was just fine. Now let me ask you this again, what..do..you..want?"

"Do you know who you're talking to?" Agent Donaldson blurted.

"Yes I do. You're point? I was asked here voluntarily. And you guys can cut the bad cop worse cop routine."

SA Johnson laughed openly, "I can see Ray why you…"

"Can we just get this done and over with?" Sheriff glared at Agent Johnson, cutting him off.

"Yes, sorry. Mrs. Yeager, what can you tell me about the days leading up to Robert asking you to marry him?"

"That's an odd question. We had been dating for about six months before he asked me. But I have known him; you know what I haven't really known him too much longer than that. I mean of course I haven't been in town for too long because I moved from Hackensack, NJ. Why do you…Oh my God. I know why you look so…" Jessica said as she fainted, right in her chair.

Both agents and the sheriff jumped right up and rushed up to her. None of them knew the cause of her fainting. The only thing they knew was that they had to make sure that Jessica was going to be ok.

SA Johnson ran out and got her some water. SA Donaldson, the younger of the two agents, just stood there looking more stupid than he already looked before Jessica passed out. And Sheriff Garcia looked like he was about to pass out himself. *Did she really just figure it out? Did she remember why I looked so familiar? Oh God please let her be ok.*

Ray was taken back to when they lived together. He remembered how he always had to prod her into eating. Even though he knew she was healthy, he always worried about her. And now that he hasn't seen her in almost 20 years, he didn't know what she had been through or what was in her past.

The great Sheriff Garcia, macho man extraordinaire, was brought to his knees, metaphorically speaking, by his heart. Even though she walked out on him so many years ago, he still felt the same he did, when he first met her. He never married, never had any children. He was waiting for that one special person that would always hold his heart. And today, destiny had intervened. Destiny smacked him upside the head and told him to wake up and look at what had been given to him, again.

Ray ever so gently brushed her hair with his hand while Jessica lay on the floor with her head on his lap. "Sheriff? Do you think we should call for an ambulance?" SA Anderson asked.

"No, just leave her alone for a little longer and if she doesn't wake up, then we can. Just wait for now." *Come on honey, wake up.* He said to himself.

Jessica's eyes started to flutter. And then out of nowhere she mumbled, "Chewy". Sheriff's heart stopped. *What the hell did she just say? Did he really hear her say the nickname that only she knew him by? Did she remember?*

"What did she just say?" SA Johnson asked.

"I don't know. I didn't catch it." Ray remarked with a big smile on his face. He knew. He knew that she subconsciously remembered him. He wanted to take her into his arms and hold her forever, but he also knew that he couldn't without the feds asking more questions than Arlen Spector.

Ray's heart was dancing so fast he felt as if he would pass out. *Come on honey wake up.* All of a sudden Jessica opened her eyes. "I'm sorry." She said ever so lightly, while looking at Sheriff Garcia. All he could muster was "I know."

"Am I missing something here?" SA Johnson asked.

"No." Ray said to Johnson. "Are you ok Jessica?"

With a smile she said "Yes I am fine. Let's just get this mess finished so I can find my daughter and try to start my life over."

"Are you sure you're ok? I mean we can do this some other time." Sheriff Garcia stated.

With a look that said it all, Ray helped her get up off the floor and back in to her chair. All he could do was keep looking at Jessica and smile. He knew he should be mad at her for the way that she left him. He knew he should be so angry that he would want nothing to do with her, but yet he couldn't. He still loved her and now that he knew that she remembered him, it just reaffirmed his belief that he made the right choice so long ago.

"Yes I am sure. Let's get this done and over with. Agent Johnson, you asked about my life with Robert. All that I can tell you is that he was very secretive and that I hadn't known him that long before we got married. He would never really talk about his life or anything from the past. And every time I would ask him any questions about it, he would get really pissed off and leave the room. Now you tell me something, what the hell is going on?"

"Well Mrs. Yeager, your so called husband is not who you think he is. Robert Yeager is not his real name. His real name is James Gaston and he has been in the witness protection program for almost 20 years. And about the only other thing I can tell you is that you might be in danger because of him."

Jessica looked as if she were going to faint again. Without even thinking, she had grabbed a hold of Ray's hand and squeezed, and wouldn't let go. Looking straight at Special Agent Johnson, she opened her mouth but couldn't force any words out.

"Jessica, would you like some water?" Sheriff Garcia asked.

"I don't, what do I, how…what am I supposed to do with this information?"

"Well first we need to make sure that you don't tell him anything. When you leave here make sure that you don't let him know that you know anything, because it's already dangerous enough for you. And if he knows that you found out about him. Well put it this way, I really don't want to have to put another person in the program."

"Agent Johnson, you mean to tell me that I have been living a lie all this time?"

"Yes that is what I am telling you. You have to keep quiet and keep a low profile."

"You dump all of this information on me and you want me to go about my life like nothing has changed? How the hell do you expect me to do that huh? You waltz into my town and turn everybody's life upside down and then want me to keep quiet? You have got one hell of a set of brass one's you know that?" Jessica yelled.

"Look lady. My partner is just trying to tell you that..." SA Donaldson.

"Excuse me? You don't talk to her like that. You're out of line SA Donaldson. She came here to talk to you out of her own volition, so unless you want your only one good thing to walk out of here, I suggest you treat Mrs. Yeager with a modicum of respect. Got it?" Sheriff Garcia blurted out. *Where the hell did that come from?*

"Agent Donaldson, your job is to be seen not heard. You understand?" Johnson asked. SA Donaldson nodded enough to make sure that Johnson seen him then looked away.

"I apologize for Agent Donaldson's outburst Mrs. Yeager. He is new and not up to agency policies. Now if you don't mind, I would like to finish what we started?"

"Agent Johnson, I have one question. What the hell did Robert do that made him one of America's Most Wanted?"

"Mrs. Yeager, you know that I can't..."

"Oh cut the bullshit Agent Johnson! You want my help; you want to know shit that could be pertinent to your case? Then you damn well better tell me something or I'm outta here. Got it? Now tell me, what the hell did he do?"

Special Agents Johnson and Donaldson looked at each other, not knowing what they should do. Should they tell her everything? Anything? If they tell her, would she still want to help them? Would she believe them? Panic set in on each of their faces.

Jessica Yeager could read their faces and tell that it was not good. Fear began to grip her stomach like a vise. *Robert was a good man.* She thought to herself. *It can't be that bad. He might not have a job but oh God help me.* Jessica grabbed Ray's hand again and braced herself.

"Mrs. Yeager, what we are about to tell you will not come easy. But whatever you think, we have back up to prove what you're about to hear." *Great another look. Damn.*

"Mrs. Yeager, your husband Robert a.k.a. James has been in the witness protection program for a good number of years because he is suspected in the rape of three women, murder of one of those women and worst off, he is wanted for the murder of Theresa LaGrassa. She is the daughter of well-known mob Godfather Anthony Mufintano, out of New Jersey. So needless to say, your life just a got a little more interesting. And the reason we are here is because we have to find him before Mufintano does."

Before the room went black Jessica could only think of one thing, *who am I?*

Chapter 6

New Jersey
Twenty years ago

James couldn't handle being told that she didn't like him or that she would never go out with him, let alone being laughed at. But there was something about Theresa LaGrassa that set him off. He knew that if she just got to know him that she would grow to love him.

James was a frequent customer at Cafe Express. He had come to know all of the staff members there. James was there almost every day buying his large double shot fat free latte, spending most of his time reading a newspaper watching everyone. But only one person really caught his eye, Theresa.

Theresa had been working there for almost as long as Café Express has been operating. Average height at 5'5 and about 155 pounds and long black hair everybody knew her. Most people liked her, or so she thought. She talked to everybody. But what she didn't know was that there was one person in particular that really liked her. He thought that if he could just get to know her, that she would make a great wife and lover.

James had been going to Café Express for a couple months watching Theresa wondering what she thought of him. Wondering if she thought of him as much as he thought of her. James loved her name, Theresa Marie LaGrassa. The thought of someone, anyone, touching her sent him to a place that he didn't want to think about. He would always sit in a corner, so as not to draw any attention to himself, but where he could see everything that was going on.

Café Express was a quaint little place. It had all of the markings of a great cafe. It had plenty of windows, which the customers loved, a few tables in the center so if there were more than four people they could gather and reminisce over old times. It had a wall full of bagels with so many choices that even Jimmy Carters head would spin. Cream cheeses, baked goods and the most important part of it all, an Espresso Bar.

Walking through the front door was the most moving thing that anybody could experience. The smells put your olfactory senses into overdrive. First thing in the morning, was always the best. Fresh coffee beans being ground for the loyal customer's lattes and fresh baked bagels going through the toaster was nothing short of heaven.

Café Express was a place where everybody could meet, relax and just enjoy themselves. It didn't matter if you were a doctor, lawyer, nurses or mechanic, everybody belonged. That is what started James on going there. First it was just a place for him to get out of the rain, but once he seen Theresa, it was all over. To James, she was the epitome of womanhood. She was something that he wasn't, outgoing, outspoken, and fun.

Who the hell was he thinking he was? James thought when he seen that guy talking to Theresa. *That was his woman. Calm down. He is just a customer. She is beautiful; maybe tomorrow would be a good time to take her to dinner. I bet she loves seafood. I bet she likes red roses.* James thought as he got up from his stool. *That's what I will do; send her a dozen red roses at work and then when I ask her she will gladly say yes to dinner.*

Walking out the door, James knew that he had her. He knew that in just a few short months, they would be married and that he would take her away from work and take care of her like she so richly deserved. James couldn't wait. It didn't matter that she didn't even know him. There are still lots of places that have arranged marriages. The husband and wife don't know each other, but yet in time they would learn to love each other.

Little did he know that his future father in law was a man that by name alone, could cause anybody to jump off the George Washington Bridge instead of being forced into any type of conversation with him.

Theresa's father was a man that you did not cross, and if you did there wouldn't be a hole deep enough for you to hide in.

"You won't get away with it. Do you know who my father is?" Theresa exclaimed.

"I don't care. You love me, you just don't know it. Once we're married, you will come to love me. I can take care of you. You don't have to work your ass off for nothing. I will make enough for both of us to be comfortable. You'll see." James stated.

"If you love me, then why do you have me tied to this chair?"

"That doesn't matter. All that matters is that you will love me."

Theresa laughed so hard that she almost tipped her chair over. "Are you fucking nuts? How could I love someone that looks like you? How could I love someone who, for starters, I don't know? You are crazy. You are certifiable. Oh my God, how did you even get along with anybody in school, let alone any girl that would cross your eye path?" Theresa kept laughing, loudly.

She never saw it coming. He hit her so hard that her head bounced off the floor when her chair tipped backwards. "Nobody laughs at me." James said.

He began pacing the floor. *Bitch! Who do you think you are? You don't laugh at people you are about to marry.* The little voice said. *Ok, deep breath. Calm down. She won't ever marry you. What did you expect? That she would run into your arms and beg you to run away with her? You're nothing. Nobody ever wanted you, so why do you think that Theresa would want you? She is somebody, you're nobody. You know what you have to do? You have to shut her up. Or she will keep laughing at you while she tells the cops what you did to her. You have no choice. Shut her up. Make her feel the pain like the pain you are feeling. You love her and she will never love you. That is the worst pain of all. Make her feel it. You know you can do it. Make her feel pain while you quiet her once and for all.*

Righting her chair, James smoothed her hair and brushed the dirt from her cheeks. "I'm sorry. I didn't mean to hit you but you gave me no choice. You're not supposed to laugh at the ones you love." Theresa just stared at James, not knowing what to think.

"James, I'm sorry you felt like you had to hit to me. But sometimes I laugh when I am nervous. Why don't you untie my hands so I can show you that I am sorry?"

Don't do it man. She will just try to run. The voice said. *She wants out. You hit her you moron, what do you expect? You have no choice now. Get rid of her. Be a man, grow some balls, and get rid of her.*

"Untie your hands? What are you thinking? It's safer this way, you'll see. Anyway I have to make sure that you fit your wedding dress. It's beautiful, you'll see. Tomorrow everything will be just perfect. And tomorrow you will see just how much I love you, when you slip that ring on your finger."

Theresa was actually getting scared now. The daughter of a reputed mob boss was scared for her life. She was sure that even her daddy couldn't get her out of this one. She had heard all kinds of stories about stalkers but never in a million years did she think that it would hit so close to home. Theresa never imagined that she would be the subject of one.

"Let me go! You can't do this. You know others will be looking for me. You know that my father will find you, and have you killed."

"I am so sick and fucking tired of hearing about your daddy. Your daddy isn't shit. He always has someone to do his dirty work for him. I doubt that you even have a daddy. You probably are just saying that to make yourself feel better, because you're scared."

"No it's true. My daddy will see you dead. You know who he is. Once he hears what you have done to me…"

"Your daddy won't do shit. Your daddy isn't shit I told you. Why do you keep lying? Hell you don't even have the same last name. What are you thinking? I'm not stupid. Tomorrow you will marry me and then it will be official. And then we are going to a place where nobody can bother us."

"Wow you really are an idiot. I told you I am not going anywhere with you…." Theresa said as she kept laughing. She laughed so hard, she caused herself to start choking.

Look at her. She is laughing at you again. You know she will never be with you. You have to do something now otherwise that bitch will win and you will always be a loser. DO IT NOW!!!

Out of nowhere he swung the machete so high and so fast that not even James was sure if it was him doing it. Blood sprayed everywhere. Theresa's head went tumbling across the floor and stopped at the old rusty door of James basement apartment. Her torso still attached to the chair, stood still save for all of the blood still pumping out of what was left of her body, dripping onto the floor.

"Oh God! Look what you made me do? How the hell am I supposed to get rid of all of this blood? What the hell where you thinking? God Theresa I am so sorry. I didn't mean to do it; it's just that you make me so crazy some times that I can't think straight."

James didn't know what to do. He didn't mean to kill Theresa. But he didn't know what to do next. *You did it. I can't believe you did it. It's about fucking time you shut that bitch up. Now all you have to do is find a place for her body and head. Nobody will know that she is gone. Hey, I know dump her body in the Hudson River and make it look like somebody else killed her because of her daddy. You could easily bury her head somewhere in the Meadowlands, that damn place is so big, nobody would find it. Problems solved. But make sure that you do it right. Then get the hell out of here and don't look back.*

James listened to the voice within. He carefully wrapped Theresa's torso in the shower curtain from his bathroom. Put her head in a garbage bag, and loaded it all into the trunk of his car.

James headed out into the dark New Jersey night not aware of the consequences of his current actions. He wasn't aware of what was about to happen to him. Nor did he know that Theresa LaGrassa's father was who she said he was. She wasn't aware that she didn't stand a chance when he met her. She didn't know that James knew who killed Theresa's mother. And James didn't know that one way or another he would not have the last word.

Chapter 7

"What are we going to do boss?" Shorty asked.

"Don't you worry about it. I know who is going to take care of that sonovabitch! He will pay for what he did to my family. Now go find Frankie and tell him that I need to talk to him."

Sitting behind his desk, Anthony began thinking "Who the fuck would be that stupid?" He never dreamed his only daughter would be raped and murdered.

Picking up the phone, he spoke into the receiver and spoke six words that would change everybody's lives in a little town in Michigan forever. "I have a job for you."

"What the hell are you talking about? Theresa moved out of town to open his new store. You know that the boss is just panicking. They don't know if it was her body. Even the news said the body was 'mummified'"

"Oh come. You can't be serious? It would be one hell of a coincidence it wasn't. The time frame fits; right around the time that Gaston left."

"Hell I read the damn news reports, I know that there was a body found in Lake Michigan years ago but the head was never recovered. How the fuck do they know that it was Theresa anyway?" Frankie blurted.

"Frankie, you obviously don't watch enough news because they just confirmed it was her. Plus if you're as smart as you say, you would know that they could do DNA testing to find out from any part of the body. They wouldn't need the head." Shorty said.

"How would the boss be able to identify he if her head wasn't attached?"

"*Dio aiutami!* Idiot."

"Whatever. All I know is that he told me to go find you because he wanted to talk to you."

"Shit. Fine. Go back over there and tell him that I will be there within an hour."

"You better, because I don't want to have to identify your body next."

Neither man said anything. They both knew what would happen to them if they didn't follow orders. Frankie Cicero, Mufitano's number one enforcer, didn't want to think about the consequences. They all knew Anthony's reputation, hell they helped build it. Frankie knew what was in store for him. He knew that him and Shorty would be the ones to carry out the death wish for whoever killed Anthony Mufitano's only daughter. The only thing that needed to be done now was to find out how that person was going to die.

"You wanted to see me boss?" Frankie asked.

"You know by now that Theresa is dead. I just got back from the morgue, it is was her that they found....."

"Yeah, I heard that there was a body found. I'm sorry to hear it was Theresa. What do you want me to do?"

"I want you to find out who did it and take care of them. I don't give a fuck what you have to do or how you do it or who gets in the way. Just take care of the sonovabitch that killed my Theresa. I already lost her mother, now her? Make...this...happen."

"Yes boss" With that order, Frankie walked out of Anthony's office and didn't look back. He knew what was expected of him, or what would happen to him if he didn't.

The Mufitano crew is well known and feared, and Anthony Mufitano was not the person you wanted to cross. His reputation preceded him. Everybody knew the type of monster he was. The citizens of East Rutherford were all afraid of him. The last time someone tried to take over his territory, it was a total blood bath. The newspapers compared the carnage to the deadly St. Valentine's Day massacre.

East Rutherford, founded in 1894, is a relatively small town in New Jersey. With a population of just over eight thousand people, East Rutherford is host to some of the most popular sports teams in the world. There are even rumors that the infamous Jimmy Hoffa was buried on the grounds of Giants Stadium in the Meadowlands.

Anthony Mufitano didn't care who knew him or who was afraid of him. All he cared about was taking care of business. His top priority right now was avenging the death of his daughter. Never did he imagine losing someone so precious. He went into a fit of rage when he lost his wife. Nobody dared to be around him, when she died.

Cecilia Mufitano was Anthony's first and only wife. He doted on her, put her on a pedestal like she was a fragile flower. Cecilia always got what she wanted but she never flaunted it. She always treated him and everybody around him like they were special. Cecilia respected everybody. She suspected that he was into some shady doings, but she didn't care. She loved him wholly.

They first met, years ago, when Cecilia was working at a diner that Anthony frequented. The minute Anthony saw Cecilia behind the counter, he was obsessed. He sent her flowers at work. Always made a point of sitting by the window, across from the cash register so he could see everything she was doing.

At first, Cecilia brushed off his advances, chalked them up to him just being overly friendly. Then he started to grow on her. Anthony was never possessive, but always made sure that she knew that he was around. She started to like the attention she was getting from him. And he in return liked her strength. He loved how she would stand up to anybody, including himself. She didn't take any shit from nobody.

Cecilia's heart was big, at times she would stay late at work to make sure even a homeless man could eat. Even if it meant she paid for it out of her own pocket. Cecilia was everybody's favorite, but when she fell in love with Anthony, he made sure that everybody knew that she was only for him. Never did she imagine that it was that love that would lead her ultimate demise.

When she asked what he did for a living, he told her that he was into investing. She never questioned him when he told her that part of his "customer service" was taking care of people who needed it. She thought he was sweet, gallant and very good looking. He thought that she was caring, fearless and beautiful. It was a match made in heaven, or hell depending on who you asked. Their whirl wind romance kept up strong and steady until the day Cecilia went to the bank to correct a problem with their account and was shot to death during a botched bank robbery.

They had been together seventeen years, married for five years and Theresa was about sixteen years old when it happened. But little did anybody know that it was not a random attack. It was a very well thought out process with an even more precise target.

Chapter 8

"Damn it. Did you two have to hit her with all of that information like that? I mean what the hell were you thinking? You better hope to God that she will be ok, or I don't care who you think you are, you will pay for what you have done to her." Ray stated.

Sheriff Garcia went back to attending to Jessica. He knew she was tough, but just how tough was she? Could she handle all of this? He couldn't bear the thought of losing her again.

Raymond Garcia was a noble man. He stood by those who deserved it and loved unconditionally. For the first time in his life, he was afraid. Not for his own life, but for someone who always held his heart. Ray lost her once, even though he didn't know why she left, he knew that it had to be bad. But if he were to lose her again, when he knows that this time he could prevent it, then he would never forgive himself.

"Tell me that you two clowns plan on making him pay one way or another for the hell he has put people through, especially Jessica?"

"Yes sheriff, he will be held accountable for his actions." Johnson said.

"Well excuse me if part of me doesn't believe you, because if that were totally true then we wouldn't be here right now."

"Sheriff, this was not our fault. The Department of Justice in charge of witness protection and…"

"Don't, don't give me excuses! You just better plan on protecting her better than the fucking President if she agrees to help you two, because if something were to happen to her…"

"We know sheriff, you've told us. Plus I know your guys history. I read your jacket. I know that you two lived together years ago, that you two were engaged and I also know that she left you, while you were going to school. I know more about you than you probably know about yourself. So trust me when I said that I will do what it takes."

For Sheriff Garcia, trust didn't come easy. And he knew that deep down; SA Johnson wasn't telling him everything. He knew about the death of Theresa LaGrassa, and a couple of unsolved rapes and deaths back in his home town. But his sixth sense was telling him that there is more to it. He just didn't know how close to home it would hit him.

"Guys, do you mind? I have a bad headache and you two aren't helping. Now, what the hell do I need to do? And another thing, I won't agree to do anything unless Sheriff Garcia is with me 24/7. You understand? Now help a lady up and let's finish talking about hell coming to town."

How much did she hear? Did she hear about the other attacks? God I hope not. I don't need her to run away from me again. Garcia thought. *I don't trust either of you, and so help me, you better not hurt Jessica or else there will be no place for you to hide.*

"Mrs. Yeager, I know you don't want to believe anything we have told you but like I said we have proof that your husband is involved, either indirectly or directly, for the rape and murders of more than one woman back in New Jersey. So we need you to help us get that information out of him." SA Johnson stated.

"If what you say is true, which I don't think so, but if what you are saying is true, are you willing to cover my ass and protect me at all the times? Do you want me in the program too? He will know. He will find out and he will probably kill me too! Robert is a suspicious man and I am not a good actor."

"Jessica, I will be with you. I will be watching you at all the times. I will not let you out of my sight ever again." Sheriff blurted.

Special Agents Johnson and Donaldson shared a look that told them that Jessica trusted Sheriff Garcia, and that he meant business. And that look also meant that they knew he was still in love with Jessica. Whatever was going to happen, this case would be handled with kid gloves.

"Mrs. Yeager, we desperately need your help, please." SA Johnson had a soft tone in his voice. It almost had a pleading sound from deep within him. But of course FBI agents were trained to control their emotions.

"Alright, fine. What the hell do you want me to do?"

"We need to set up a time for you to come in to be wired. Is there any time in the day that your husband is not at home or that you step out to do something?"

"You're an asshole you know that? She is afraid for her life and you're putting a wire on her? *Robert better hope that the mob gets to him first. Sheriff or not, I will make sure that he pays for what he did to everybody, especially Jessica.*

"Sheriff! Talk to me like that again, and I will have you escorted out of here!" SA Johnson yelled.

"Fuck you. You don't have the authority to have me escorted out of here. Threats don't work on me Johnson. And you couldn't drag me out of here with the National Guard, so you better be on your best behavior. Or I will find a way to take care of Robert myself. Got it?"

Both men were now standing nose to nose, ready to throw off their gloves. Even though they were on the same side, Sheriff Garcia was ready to fight to protect what was his. He didn't care that he just made a threat in front of two FBI agents. All he cared about was keeping his rediscovered love. And he would stop at nothing to protect her.

"Will you two stop acting like school yard bullies and sit the hell down? You are both supposed to be on the same side, remember? Ray," Jessica said as she faced him and grabbed his arm, "You need to know that this is something I have to do. I need to know if I married the wrong man."

That comment shocked Garcia out of his testosterone revere. He took a deep breath and exhaled like a deflated balloon. He knew at that moment, that she still loved him. *You don't understand I can't lose you again.* He thought. "Fine but if Agent SuperFreak here lets anything, and I mean anything happen to you I will make sure that Mueller himself will bring him up on charges!"

Both men sat down and began talking about what had to be done and when. Wiring Jessica was going to be a tedious affair. Not only was she nervous when she walked in, but knowing that she was about to set her husband up made it worse. As much as Sheriff Garcia hated the idea he knew that it had to be done, for more than one reason.

"Ok Mrs. Yeager, as I said before, we need to come up with a time that would work for all of us. Will there be a time that would work better for you?"

"Actually there is. Robert will end up going to Malone's Pub tomorrow morning. And he will be there for couple of hours. That's where he spends most of his time at the bar."

"Good, good. What time?"

"I can be here after I get Cassie off for school, so how about 8 am?"

"Ok that will work. I will have my team meet me here at 7 am to get everything ready for your arrival. Do you want us or Sheriff Garcia to pick you up?"

"What have you been smoking? Just what I need is you two or a cop car showing up at my front door. Yeah sure, that won't give my neighbors or anybody else something to talk about. Hell, what if someone else is watching, huh? Do you think I want to die young? No thanks. I will find my own way here."

"Sorry, you're right. We will wait for you here." SA Johnson apologized.

They might not give a shit, but I will make sure that you're safe and watched. Garcia thought.

With the meeting over, SA Johnson, Agent Donaldson, Jessica and Sheriff Garcia walked outside to their waiting cars.

"Sheriff, Mrs. Yeager, we will see you tomorrow." SA Johnson said as he shook their hands.

The two 'Super Agents' walked to their cars and Sheriff Garcia watched Jessica out of the corner of his eye as she started to walk to her car parked next to the agents car. "Jessica, I promise, I will not let anything happen to you. I know you blame me for the way things ended years ago, but I want you to know that I still…"

Just then the ground shook as Sheriff Garcia and Jessica were thrown back. After what seemed like a lifetime, Sheriff Garcia got back to his feet, checked to make sure that Jessica was alright and ran to the agents' car. But there was nothing that he could do because what used to be the car was now an inferno, with the two agents burning alive inside.

"Sheriff, what the hell was that?" The desk sergeant asked as he and about ten other cops came running out.

"That was a message I'm afraid."

Sheriff Garcia, in all of his years of training, never expected for his little town to be targeted, never expected to be in the cross-hairs of hell.

Chapter 9

"Agent Ritter, what have you found so far? Director Colbert asked.

"Well sir, I know that he is in Michigan. I know that he is going by the name of Robert Yeager. He is married to Jessica, former Greer, and has one step-daughter named Cassie. From what I have been able observe he is not making too many friends. If we don't do something soon, it might be too late. Gaston is a loose cannon and I am afraid someone is going to light the fuse."

"Do you know anything else?" "My partner says that Yeager is a true piece of work. He is not liked by his neighbors. He is not a big guy, kind of wiry. Physically and mentally abuses those around him. He is a control freak and seems to have a strong hold on Jessica."

"If I wasn't in this office or in the position I am in I would be tempted to just let Mufintano take him and not worry about it."

"Sir?" "Nothing. Never mind. We need to do something about him before Mufintano gets to him or anybody else for that matter. Keep a close eye on him until we have enough evidence to hold him."

"You plan on bringing him in? I mean that has never been done has it? Arresting someone in the program? What kind of shit will we get if we do arrest him?"

"Who the hell knows? But there is one thing that I do know, if we don't bring him in we will be in a world of hurt from all sides, including the wrong side. So let's just keep a close eye on him for right now and pray."

"Yes sir. One more thing sir."

"Yeah what?" "I think that there is more to my partner than he is letting on. I haven't figured it out yet but something isn't right with him."

"Should I be worried?"

"I don't think so. I just feel like he has a deeper investment in this whole Gaston issue."

"Do you think they know who Gaston really is?" "He has to know. I mean those two other agents were just blown up in front of him. They had plans on having Gaston's wife being wired."

"If you get scared, call me and I will have a team extract you and send someone else in."

"No way sir! You couldn't drag me away. Besides, Cassie is the key to my success."

"I am not going to ask what the hell you mean by that. Do not get yourself too close agent. You are there to serve one purpose, watch Gaston. You understand? Do not allow yourself to get personally involved. Got it?"

"Yes sir. I understand, don't worry. I have no interest in Cassie Damian, I assure you."

"You better not. We can't afford to have you compromise this case because you have fallen for a potential suspect."

"Sir, I will be fine. You do know that if you keep squinting like that your brow will become permanently scarred? You are a much better looking man when you smile!" Agent Ritter said while fighting to keep a straight face.

"Look smart ass, you don't worry about my brow. You just worry about you doing your job."

"Yes sir!" Agent Ritter said as he saluted Director Colbert while knotting his eyebrows.

"Get out of here before you piss me off even more."

"Yes sir." Agent Ritter walked out of Director Colbert's office, but not before winking at him.

The whole agency is looking out for a man who should be dead. How the hell has he made it this far? Nobody knew the answer to that question. Even the FBI couldn't explain why James Gaston was still on this planet. Yes things do happen for a reason but usually to good people. Why to this man? Why for so long?

James Gaston had eluded death for a long time while racking up death points across the US. There are so many people who wanted him dead that even the Vatican couldn't keep track.

Agent Eric Ritter, new to the agency, had been picked for this assignment because of his boyish charm. His boy next door looks and his ability to get almost anybody to talk to him would not be enough for this specific assignment. Agent Ritter would find himself in a mess that even he couldn't dig himself out of even with the help of John Douglas.

"I am here for an interview with Troy." AJ said.

"Hold on a moment, I will see if he is back yet." Taryn said. She proceeded to go around and find Troy.

Troy Decker was the son of the owner of Rosie's Café. A nice little coffee shop nestled back just off the main road in North Muskegon. It opened early in the morning and closing after dark, with a combination of interesting customers and employees; there is never a dull moment.

Troy is an interesting creature himself; a good looking young man, clean shaven, slender and about 6 foot tall. Troy gets ogled a lot by the female employees but he definitely dishes it out too. He is good natured and barely lets anything get to him. 25 years old one would never guess that his maturity level is that of a 50 year old.

"Hi. I'm Troy, have a seat so we can get this thing started."

"Hi. My name is AJ. I just recently moved into the area from Washington and I am just looking into making a fresh start. I can work any hours that you would like, day or night. I do have my own transportation; I know that's pretty important with most employers. I don't have any major life issues, I am single with no kids, no personal problems and ready to start when you need me."

"Well I do have a couple of questions. Have you ever worked in any type of restaurant setting before?"

"Yes I have. I worked at a place similar to this, SBC. I don't know if you have ever heard of it, but it is all in my resume."

"Actually, I haven't but that doesn't mean anything. My uncle is a cop with the sheriff's department so I can use him to check out anything."

"Good. It's nice to have those kind of connections. I always wanted to be a cop but my mom had other plans for me. You said there were two questions, what is the other one?"

"When can you start?"

"Wow you work quick."

"Yeah. I have to be honest. We are very short staffed and need someone yesterday. I will still be checking on your background but everything seems ok here. Come in tomorrow about 8:30 am and I will get you your uniform and all the necessary paperwork."

"Ok thanks, I will do that."

With all of that being said, the two shook hands and Troy went back into his office. In the parking lot on way her car AJ's cell phone rang. "Hello?"

"How did the interview go?"

"I'm in. I start tomorrow. Tell the boss that everything is good to go and I will report later. Tell him that I will call him tomorrow after work."

"Ok, will do. One thing, you better watch your ass. With everything that has been stirred up, anything can happen."

"I know. Contrary to what everybody thinks, I can take care of myself. I will not let the boss down. See ya."

After that brief phone call, AJ shook it off, got into her car and lit a cigarette. What had she gotten herself into? She wasn't that young but yet she sure as hell wasn't that old either. Knowing how most of this hinged on her, AJ hoped her nerves could hold up. But one thing for sure, if she made one wrong move, she would be taking a permanent nap at the bottom of the Hudson.

Chapter 10

"Sheriff? Sheriff! Are you ok? What the hell happened? Sheriff!" the desk sergeant yelled, while other officers ran toward the burning car. It was futile, the car was blown to pieces and the agents inside were no more.

Sheriff Garcia shook his head and proceeded to force himself up off the concrete. Nobody saw this coming. Somebody wanted this investigation stopped, but whom? Sheriff Garcia had no clue.

The desk sergeant grabbed Sheriff Garcia by the shoulder and spun him around so they were looking each other in the eye. "Sheriff, are you ok?"

"Sonovabitch." Garcia exclaimed.

"Sheriff are you hurt?" Sgt Harris asked.

"I'm fine. Get the damn bomb squad here now and find out who the hell just killed these agents and tried to kill my contact."

"Sheriff?"

"What?!"

"What contact?"

"Where the hell is Jessica?"

"Sheriff, what contact, who are you talking about? Who is Jessica?"

"The only link we have to blowing this case apart. If we lose her we might as well kiss our ass's good bye. Find her now!"

Sheriff Raymond Garcia had never been so scared in his life. He never thought he would find her again. Then when Jessica walked into his life without notice, declared her love for him, he thought he had been dreaming.

The thought of losing her again, possibly for good, put Sheriff Garcia in a place that he didn't want to go to again. Sheriff Garcia was normally a happy go lucky person, but facing the prospect of losing half of his heart was not a good thing. If Raymond Garcia lost Jessica, hell would be a better place to live.

"Sheriff, we just did a search of the area and we can't find nobody else, dead or alive. I don't know what to tell you but if your contact is still alive after that blast she is gone."

"We have to find her, because if I'm right about who is involved in this, she won't stand a chance."

"Sheriff, what is going on here? I mean, this town went from quiet and boring to everybody scared for their lives. What the hell is going on here?"

"All I can tell you is that there are some very dangerous people involved and they will stop at nothing to make sure that this case does not get solved. My contact is the only direct link to blowing this whole case wide open and if something happens to her, it's over."

"We'll find her sheriff."

"I'll fucking kill him if anything happens to Jessica. He won't stand a chance. If he thinks that he puts fear into his victims, he doesn't know shit. I will make him wish he that he had stayed in Jersey."

"Sir?"

"Never mind, call the Crime Scene Unit and have them thoroughly investigate this crime scene. Something is wrong. If I'm right, she is close and he is watching us right now. He wants to watch us run scared. He wants to think that he is controlling everything, including what happens next. I'll be damned if I will let him do that. But, right now we have to let him think that he is pulling all the strings. If he even suspects that we know what's going on, we will lose her for sure."

"Who the hell is he? Who has Jessica? Sheriff you have to tell us what the hell this is all about so we can help you? We can't do this blind. It wouldn't be safe. Damn it sheriff you need to tell us. Who wants this town run on fear? Sheriff, you have to take a deep breath and tell us, now."

"Anthony Mufintano."

"The New Jersey mob boss?"

"Yes. I'm not completely sure on all of the details but all I know is that he came here looking for someone and Jessica is the wife of the soon to be dead man that has been here hiding under the Witness Protection Program. She agreed to help us, the FBI and the Department of Justice because her husband did some shit that Mufintano didn't like. Now she is gone and so help me God…"

"Sheriff why didn't you tell us sooner? We could have coordinated something so this wouldn't have happened."

"Coordinated something? What the hell do you think you could have prepared for with this? Did you fucking see this one coming, because I sure as hell didn't? Anyway, I just found out all of this today. So don't try to make me feel better by reminding me how fucked up things really are right now. Alright?"

"Sorry sir. But this is just one hell of a wake-up call for everybody. Now what do you want us to do next?"

"Get Jessica and get Mufintano. I want to make sure that he knows who is boss when this is all over."

"Sheriff one question, I understand that you are concerned for your witness's safety but the extra added interest in her. Why do you care about her so much?"

"Don't worry about it; just make sure that she survives this so Mufintano can pay for turning my town into World War III."

It didn't take long before Mufintano walked in to the room. "What the hell do you think you're doing? I didn't tell you to hurt her. If you touch her again, you will have to deal with me. *Capiche?* Mrs. Yeager, are you ok? I promise that they will not touch you again. If you cooperate with me and my men I will let you go. Now, do you want or need anything? Some water perhaps?"

All Jessica Yeager could do was shake her head no. She was too terrified to even think. One minute she was walking out of the sheriff's department with the love of her life and the next thing she was being picked up off the ground and thrown into a van. There was no time to think about anything, all she could do was hope and pray that she would make it out alive.

"Shorty, give her some water and be nice about it."

"Yes boss."

Shorty Santoro walked over to what looked like a sink and turned the faucet on, not knowing that there was no water pressure. After much mumbling, Shorty was able to get Jessica something to drink.

The warehouse was dark and cold, with wind coming from every direction through the clapboard siding. It resembled an old meat packing plant, with old broken down rusted grinding machines. Large meat hooks hanging from the center of the room. In the corner, a white rusty door with a large metal handle that said no entry that leads to who knows where. It was not a happy bright place.

Jessica was tied to a folding chair in the middle of the room, hands tied behind her back, her mouth covered back up with duct tape and tears streaming down both cheeks. All she could do was pray and wonder how the hell she got there. Having just found out that the man she was married to, was not who he pretended. Robert Yeager a.k.a. James Gaston was an evil man who brought danger on himself and those around him. It wasn't until now that Jessica realized the man she really loved was probably dead because of the explosion, and it was her fault. She thought that if she had just walked away, none of this would have happened.

"Mrs. Yeager, you have to tell me where to find your husband. See, he took something of infinite value from me a long time ago and I will make him pay. I do not want to hurt you, but if your husband doesn't show….." Mufintano said as he carefully removed the tape from Jessica's mouth.

"Look I don't know who you are but I promise if you let me go I will find him for you."

"Yeah, ok. Let's say I believe you, how do you know that you will be able to find him?" Mufintano said as he put the loaded Beretta Cougar to her head.

"Because he is an alcoholic and they are predictable. And right now aside from being scared shitless, I am incredibly pissed off right now. I can help you if you let me. I don't know what he did to you and I don't really care. All I do know is that I want out of here alive. So please give me a chance, and we both might benefit."

"Do you think I am a fucking idiot? I didn't get where I am by listening to people like you. Now, before I really get pissed off, tell me where your husband is or I will not hesitate to pull the damn trigger!"

"No…God…please, don't I don't know where he is right now, I swear. But I know I can find him. Please don't." Jessica pleaded as Mufintano cocked the Beretta.

"You have about 30 seconds to tell me what I want to know before I kill you."

Screaming at the top of her lungs, "I told you I don't know where…."

All of a sudden everything exploded in a bright light and one of the walls came tumbling down. Before anybody knew it, there was gun fire everywhere. Mufintano and his men scrambled like cockroaches when the lights are turned on, but not before Mufintano took a round in the shoulder, as Jessica was screaming in terror.

"Everybody freeze!" Garcia screamed, along with the other members of the sheriff's department and the SWAT team.

More gun fire erupted as police were screaming for Mufintano and his crew to stand still. Nobody listened as they ran for cover. Garcia knew he missed his chance at capturing Mufintano and ending this catastrophic war, but he also knew that Mufintano had been hit and Shorty Santoro lay dead in a pool of his own blood and at Jessica's feet.

There was no movement, no sounds that emerged from Jessica. "Jessica. Jessica! Don't you die on me damn it. I've waited too long to lose you now." Crouching down to ear level, while checking for a pulse, Ray whispered in her ear, "I love you, don't you dare die on me."

"You can't get rid of me that easy."

Lifting Jessica's chin Ray chuckled, "I hate you right now you know that don't you?"

"No you don't, you just said you loved me."

"I need an ambulance in here now!" Sheriff barked.

Raymond Garcia knew that this wasn't over. Mufintano and most of his crew were unaccounted for. They were out there somewhere planning their next move. Garcia knew that they should all be afraid, for he knew that this was just the calm before the storm. Mufintano would not be deterred by this set back. He would strike again, only this time like a cornered.

Chapter 11

"Jessica, are you ok? Have you been shot? There is blood all over you?"

"I'm fine. The blood isn't mine. Look I'm sorry. I didn't mean for you to get hurt."

"What are you talking about? This is not your fault. You didn't ask to get abducted. You didn't ask to be tricked into marrying a sociopath. You did nothing to deserve any of this! You understand me?"

"That's not what I meant."

"Why didn't you ever tell me? I was sick when you left. I couldn't believe that you just up and left. I thought something happened to you. Why? Why did you leave me? What did I ever do to you to deserve this?" Ray yelled.

"Chewy look at me. I loved you with all my heart. I still do. But after what I went through, I couldn't face you."

"What you went through? Where do you get off? I went through hell looking for you, worrying about you."

"You just don't get it. You never will. I am sorry. I did what I had to do. Put it this way, I would rather die than live without you. But I had to leave, he just….never mind I don't expect you to believe anything I say right now. Just know that no matter what I will always love you." Jessica said as she turned and began walking away. She had no intention of spilling the beans to him. She vowed to herself that she would never tell him the real reason as to why she left him 18 years ago.

"I wanted you to be my wife. I wanted us to grow old together. Would that have been so terrible? Why didn't you love me?"

Without turning around, Jessica tears streaming down her face, finally laid out the reason for her difficult decision so many years ago. "Damn it Ray, I was raped! There now you know the truth. Now you have a reason to leave me. That's why I did it Ray, I just beat you to the punch. I left first."

In all his years of being cop, it never prepared him for hearing that. Sheriff Raymond Garcia, public official extraordinaire, was just brought down by fear and love. All this time he thought that she didn't love him. All this time he thought he wasn't good enough. He never imagined that the love of his life, the other half of his heart, left him to save him from the pain of humiliation. He never thought that she had been so afraid of what happened to her that she couldn't face him.

"Why didn't you tell me? I loved you no matter what. Why didn't you trust me enough to handle something like that?"

"Ray, you stand there and look at me and tell me that you wouldn't have left me? You were on your way to greater things. You didn't need that extra baggage."

"How dare you think that you can choose for me what I can handle and what I can't? That is not for you to decide. I loved you, I still do. But I guess my love wasn't enough, was it?"

"You're right, it wasn't fair. But I couldn't bear the thought of having you have to deal with my shame. I couldn't barely deal with it myself let alone ask someone else to shoulder that burden too."

"I told you that was not up to you. Don't you think I should be the one to decide what I can or cannot deal with? Tell me one thing, is Cassie my daughter?"

The silence said it all. Ray knew at that point that Cassie was his daughter; Jessica didn't have to tell him anything.

"I wasn't sure. I just realized that I missed my period when I was attacked and just made an appointment with a doctor for the pregnancy test. And then you proposed. And the next day after walking home from work......" Jessica started to sob uncontrollably. "Chewy I am so sorry for ever hurting you. I was scared. I just didn't know how you would react. I just didn't know what to do. God I am sorry." Jessica just collapsed and sat on nearest thing, the bed of Ray's truck.

Ray just stood there in disbelief, not knowing what to do or what to say. But that only lasted a second. Ray sat down next to Jessica and took her in to his arms and embraced her like it was her last moment on Earth.

While Jessica laid her head on Ray's shoulder, he began stroking her hair. "Honey, I love you. Probably more than you will ever know, and I promise I will not let anything or anybody ever hurt you again. I don't know where we go from here but I will always be here for you. You have to believe that."

That just made Jessica cry even more. She knew or she hoped that Ray loved her but she never really knew how much until just now. He could have run away when she told him the truth about that night. But instead he stayed to make sure that she was ok. He could have gotten mad and yelled, called her a liar, but instead he stayed to comfort her, because he loved her.

Ray didn't let her see the lone tear that rolled down his cheek. It was up to him to stay strong for her because of all these years of hell that she had kept bottled up inside of her. For all of the times that Jessica had to wake up alone. For all of the times that she had to be the only one to go to Cassie's school functions or explain to her why her father wasn't around.

The worst part of it all, the thing that was killing him the most, was not knowing that he had a daughter. So many emotions were roiling inside Ray. Yet, he felt like he owed it to her to be strong; for all of the times that she was alone with nobody to talk to when it really mattered the most. For not being there for his daughter when she needed him. He knew he didn't have time to beat himself up about anything. Right now he had to figure out what his next step was going to be.

"Jessica, we need to get you to the hospital and have you checked over to make sure that you are ok. I don't want you to worry, I will take care of you like I should have done so many years ago. I will make sure that whoever did this; will not get away with it. I promise that. You will stay with me until this threat is over, and I will not take no for an answer."

Of all the times that the good sheriff was ever afraid, it never felt like this. He felt sick to his stomach, he felt like adrenaline was in overload. Ray never thought he could be so confused, hurt and angry all in one. But most of all, he was angry over everything that was going on. Angry, about his town being ripped apart because of one man. Angry over the loss of two agents, angry at coming so close to losing Jessica but most of all, he wanted to do serious damage to that one man he took away his loves innocence away so many years ago.

Sheriff Garcia would do anything in his power to make sure nobody ever got hurt again. As Ray and Jessica got in to his truck and headed for the hospital, Ray had a twisted thought form into his brain. *I am the sheriff; nobody would question anything I did. I could make it look like an accident.* Ray squeezed her hand as he held it and thought *I am not losing Jessica again, ever.*

Chapter 12

"Daphne, we have to take that chance. You just don't get it. Two FBI agents got blown up in their own car, in front of the police station no less. And the only reason I know is because the sheriff assigned that investigation to me. Somebody has gone to great lengths to make sure that whatever secret is out there doesn't get out. I mean who the hell is willing to kill agents without thinking?"

"I have no idea but I'll be damned if I am going to let them get to Brandie. You might not give a shit about her but I do."

"Don't fucking give me that holier than thou attitude, you just found out about her; just like you just found me. What makes you so damn sure that it is her? Look I have work to do. Is there anything else you want to chat about sis, or can I get my shit done?"

"Butch whether you like it or not, you are no longer an only child. Now you can get used to it and deal with it or you can go about your lonely, miserable life and act like nothing ever happened. Either way, that's not going to change the fact that somebody wants people dead, including our sister Brandie. No matter, I am going to talk to her and pray that she will listen to me, before it's too late."

Daphne turned towards the door and started to walk out of the police garage. But before she made it to the door Butch spun her around and stopped her. "Look Daphne, this is all new to me. I was raised an only child just like you and Brandie. So excuse me if I seem a little put off and aren't jumping for joy at having siblings. When did you plan on going to talk to her and exactly what were you planning on saying to her?"

"I don't know. I haven't really gotten that far yet but I do know that I will not let James ruin another life. That man has destroyed too many people in the course of twenty or more years. He needs to be stopped for good."

"What are you going to do Daphne?"

"I don't know. I have to do something before it's too late, before someone else winds up dead."

"Alright fine, call me after 5 pm when I get out of work so we can meet. I'm not promising anything, but you're right, something needs to be done. I just hope that it's not too late."

Daphne turned around and walked out of the garage. Neither of them had any clue as to the gravity of it all. Neither Daphne nor Butch knew what was about to follow. They didn't realize that they were about to enter a level of hell that would make even Charles Manson jealous.

While Daphne was driving home, she began thinking about her new found family. The diary of her mothers', with an envelope in it, she found while going through the house after her mother died.

> *Dear Daphne,*
>
> *I know this is not the way that I envisioned telling you about my past and your future. But I hope that someday you can bring yourself to forgive me for not telling you when I was alive. I am sorry if you are reading this, my disease has run its course and that you must be going through the house to get it ready to sell.*
>
> *I know that by now you are wondering what was so secretive that I had to keep it from you and everybody else but I was too ashamed to tell anyone. I know that you have grown up to be a beautiful young lady. You just need to know that you are a strong willed woman who can do anything once you set your mind to it. Ok I guess I can't avoid it any longer. Please forgive me for what I am about to tell you.*
>
> *One night after I had gone to the grocery store, I was walking across the parking lot to my car and a stranger*

approached me while I was getting ready to unlock my door. Oh, it was dark. I didn't have my keys ready and the next thing I knew I was being kicked around on the pavement while I tried to protect my head. Then he forced me on my back and raped me. By that point I was too weak to fight back or even yell for help. I was so helpless and scared; I just laid there and prayed to God that he would kill me so it would be over.

The next thing I knew I was waking up in the hospital staring out of one eye at a nurse who looked like Robin Williams in a dress. I couldn't hardly remember anything, couldn't talk, hell I didn't remember who I was for a moment. I think it was one of the scariest moments I ever experienced. Not knowing who I was is something I wouldn't wish on anybody.

It was about month later when I realized that I missed my period. By then I was alone and afraid to leave my house. I did the best I could at forgetting that night and raising you like nothing happened. I am so sorry for never telling when you became old enough. I am sorry for not trusting you with this. It's just that I wanted to save you from the pain of knowing where you came from.

You are and will always be the best thing that ever happened to me, you have to know that. You saved me. Before you came along, I didn't know where I was going in life and now that I am dying I'm just sorry that we never got the chance to really talk. I love you so much and am so sorry for never being there for you, for never having the courage to tell you.

I hope that one day you can forgive me. You will make a beautiful bride some day; I am just so sorry that I will never get the chance to see it happen. You need to know that I have faith in knowing you will make it on your own. All you have to do is believe. I love you honey. I will always be around; I will always be there for you if you just believe.

I love you always,
Mom

Daphne, full of tears, could barely see to keep herself on the road. She hated to read that letter and feel the torment in her mother's words. She couldn't hate her mother. It didn't matter to her where she came from, just knowing how much her mother loved her and did everything from her heart was enough to keep Daphne's mother's memory alive in her.

Pulling into her parking spot at her apartment, Daphne reached for her cell phone to make that dreadful call to her newly found brother. All she could do was hope that Butch would be a willing participant in stopping a monster. But unbeknownst to her, Daphne was going to find out just how close to her new brother she really is.

Chapter 13

Brandie knew she had to do something to stop Robert. She wasn't sure exactly what he was doing to everybody, especially Cassie but she knew it wasn't good. After spending more time with AJ and talking with her she felt as if she could confide in her.

Brandie told AJ that she was going to send a letter to her aunt in Nuremburg, Germany and she in turn was supposed to send it back to the sheriff department. In the letter, it would tell them just exactly what type of person Robert was and it would also tell the police what exactly he was doing to her best friend Cassie.

AJ was new to the area, she was a transplanted Michiganian. Originally from Virginia, AJ was a tom boy at heart. But she was also secretive. She kept to herself, but when she befriended someone, she would go out of her way for them.

Brandie and AJ hit it off instantly. The more AJ worked the more she and Brandie talked. They were often seen going out together. They weren't as close as Brandie and Cassie but they did get close. But there was something that Brandie didn't know about AJ, something that when everybody found out, the shock effect would make it truly unbelievable.

One day while they were having breakfast together, Brandie accidentally let it slip that her best friend was being tortured by her step father in more than one way. She also told AJ that she wanted to do something about it but she was afraid that nobody would believe her because she was just a 'kid'.

AJ told Brandie that she should try anyway because somebody like him needs to be treated in the same sick way as those he hurt. "Brandie, you need to do something about him. Robert shouldn't get away with abusing your friend or anybody for that matter. What did you plan to do to make people listen to you? I mean who are you going to approach to make them listen?"

"I don't know, I just know that I have to do something. Robert needs to be stopped. He gives me the creeps. I can't explain it, maybe it's the way he looks at me or others when I see him but there is something not right with him."

"Couldn't you go to the police? I would think that they would listen to you."

"And say what? 'Sheriff, I need to tell you that my best friend is being abused by her step father, you need to do something about it.' He won't listen to me. Nobody will."

"You never know unless you try Brandie. How are you going to feel if something happens to her and you stood back and did nothing?"

"Nice pep talk there AJ, thanks."

"I'm sorry honey but you know that I'm right. Look, someone like Robert only thinks about himself. He gets off on control and power. He gets off by scaring and controlling, but once you take that power away from him, he can't be scary anymore. One more question, what makes you so sure that he is doing this anyway?"

"Are you serious? Why would I lie about something like that?"
"I didn't mean that you are lying. I meant how bad it is. I mean you can't be there with her every minute."

"You're right. I can't be there every minute. You don't know what this guy is like. He's creepy, he's constantly watching her. He's married and he always wants to be with her more than his wife. There is just something about him that people don't trust including me and my parents. He's not right."

"Ok, look if you want some help with this whole situation then you have to let me help you."

"Like how? How you are going to help me when I can't get people to believe me. The cops aren't going to do shit, I told you."

"Trust me; I can get people to listen to me; even if I have to put a gun to their heads. Meet me after work tomorrow and I will help you write the letter you are going to send to your aunt in Germany."

"Where do you want to meet?" "I know I can give you a ride home after work and we can go to your house." "Fine maybe then you will get look at Robert and you can judge for yourself what his is like."

"Ok but I can tell you right now, I don't like this. I don't like how this sounding. Tell me one thing, how close do you live to him?"

"You'll love this. He lives right across the street from me."

With an exasperated look on her face AJ blurted out, "You're shitting me?"

"No I'm not. Why the hell do you think that I constantly want to be away from the area? It wouldn't surprise me if that sick bastard was looking at me through a pair of binoculars getting off."

"Look I will help you anyway I can with this guy, but you have to be careful. You don't want to let him know that you're watching him. If he finds out, he will more than likely change his daily patterns. And then you will never be able to prove anything."

"Are you sure that you're just a kid? I mean sometimes you don't act like one."

"I'm sorry but I have had a rough life, I've learned the hard way with a lot of shit."

"Ok, you can give me a ride home tomorrow and we can talk more then."

"Great see you then. Talk to you tomorrow."

AJ and Brandie parted ways. The whole time Brandie was thinking about what she was going to say in the letter to her aunt she was going to send and make its way back to the sheriff. She had no clue where she was going to start. She didn't know what to say, but she had to do something to stop him. Little did Brandie know, that she was playing right in to the hands of the one person who could stop Robert in his tracks.

"I'm supposed to meet her tomorrow after work. I am giving her a ride home and she wanted my input on what she should do to stop Robert. Yeah I know that she is just a kid, but that shouldn't matter. He deserves to pay for what he did. I don't care about anything else but seeing him pay. I'm not getting too close. No, I'm doing that. I'm helping her. Just back off and let me do my damn job. I'm not going to let

him hurt anybody else. I think that he should be tortured like those he tortured. Don't worry; I won't do anything that I can't get out of. Whatever, I gotta go. Bye."

Hanging up her cell phone, AJ thought about the earlier conversation with Brandie. She knew that if she wasn't careful she could get herself in deep. AJ never thought that her boss was going to be that concerned considering he made a living out of hurting people. AJ knew she had to help Brandie before it was too late. If Robert kept doing what he was doing to good people, no telling what would happen next.

Chapter 14

He could see him from the tree where he was sitting. He knew that in just one second Robert wouldn't be causing any more pain to others. The fall winds weren't too bad. He didn't worry about falling but he was more concerned about missing.

Robert has to die, he thought to himself. *Nobody knows I'm here, they would never suspect a thing*. He could shoot him, quietly, and get back to his life as it was before that monster surfaced. He knew that nobody else was going to take things into their own hands. They wouldn't have the guts to take out the man that so many hated.

All it was going to take was one single shot, no evidence. There would be no sound heard, for he was up high in a tree and it was in the middle of the night and everybody was fast asleep.

The crossbow was the perfect weapon of choice. Quick, painless, and to the point but why should Robert get off so easy? He inflicted so much pain on so many innocent people, if he didn't feel any pain how would that be fair?

A shot from this distance, could be tricky but not for him. He was an expert hunter, a perfect shot. A hundred yards isn't much for someone like him especially if he knew Robert would sit still long enough to take the shot through the rickety old window.

His nerves felt like steel and nothing was going to change his mind. He knew that if he was going to do anything to stop Robert that it had to be done soon. The only thing that concerned him was the thought of getting caught. He couldn't live without his family that he loved so much. But he took solace in the fact that Robert wouldn't be hurting anybody else.

He righted his body, steadied himself so there would be no chance of falling and brought the crossbow up. The cross-hairs never looked so beautiful on anybody before until now. Who would blame him for killing Robert? Anybody? There isn't any one person who hasn't been affected by him.

I am doing the right thing, I know it. I can't stop now. Robert is a monster who doesn't know what it's like to care. Why the hell should it matter if he died anyway? That man is a complete psychopath with no conscious. He doesn't care who he hurts. He needs to be stopped, plain and simple.

He knew with every passing minute the longer it took before Robert died, the longer it would be before his life would be back in order. He loved life and most of all he loved his job. Once it was over, Robert would be no more. Once it was over, hell would be no more.

Not knowing anything about the people around you also makes it hard to trust anybody. As bad as Daphne yearned for the feeling of closeness from family she still wasn't sure what to do or who she could truly turn to. The only thing for sure was that she had a brother and a sister and somebody out there wasn't playing by the rules.

Daphne was daydreaming about her soon to be new husband and where she wanted to go on their honeymoon but even though she tried to distract herself it wasn't working too well. *What the hell am I going to do? Butch doesn't give a shit.* She thought to herself.

Looking out the window of her kitchen Daphne thought she saw movement out in the nicely manicured lawn. But in a subdivision anything is possible, anything can move and sometimes does. *He knows better, he can't get away with it,* she thought. Daphne never thought that she would have worry about being safe in her own home.

While still in college, Daphne landed a good job in a law office as a paralegal until she got her law degree. Young, beautiful and smarter than people give her credit for, she had everything going for her. Life was good until it took an unexpected detour.

But one thing that was for certain, Daphne had family and one of those family members was in need of her help. Even though her sister doesn't know that she existed, she wouldn't have to handle it on her own. If Butch wasn't going to help she was bound and determined to do something.

"Who the hell did she think she was anyway? I was just fine by myself, not having to worry about anybody but me damn it! I don't fucking need anybody hovering over me. Sonovabitch!" Butch thought to himself. The more he thought, the more he wondered if it could be true or not.

While working on the exploded federal car Butch wondered, *'How the hell am I supposed to know if she's telling the truth? I don't know her, neither of them. I don't know anything about this supposed Robert. Why should I fucking care? I was doing just fine by myself before she came in and interrupted my life. Sonovabitch.'* Battling the thoughts within him, Butch had a sense of decency. He knows that if he didn't at least check things out. He would feel awful if it came out that it was true and did nothing.

Getting his attention back to the car, he found something that made him wonder if it could all be true or not. *'Now why would a watch be taped to the starter?'* Butch knew something was off and he knew he had to call the sheriff to tell him what he found.

"Sheriff, we have a problem. Whatever is going on here is bigger than we all expected. And I think you should get over here to the garage as soon as possible. Whoever did this, knows what they were doing. Alright, see you in a few."

Butch hung up the phone and his mind was racing; was Daphne telling the truth, why would his parents lie to him about his childhood and who is behind wreaking havoc on his favorite town. Most of all he wondered, who would be next.

Chapter 15

She wasn't sure what she was doing on the floor. She couldn't remember how she got there or where the blood on her hands came from. All she did remember was getting a real bad headache before blacking out.

She wanted to find her mother and to tell her that she had another episode. But when she put her arms behind to get up searing pain shot right up her right shoulder. *Sonovabitch!* What the hell? Why did her shoulder hurt so damn bad, she thought to herself? Putting most of her weight on her left arm, she finally got the strength to stand up. It was then she realized that her legs were weak, wobbly and wondered if she was going to be able to stay standing.

"Mom." she yelled. When no one answered, she thought that was odd and set out to try and see if her mom was home. Putting one foot in front of the other, she slowly walked out of her bedroom and down the hall of the small, shoddy built trailer to see where her mother was.

Why was there blood on the floor in the hall? She thought to herself.

The trailer was old, and very small. Sized like a can for sardines, the trailer had two very small bedrooms one on each end, a bathroom, kitchen-diningroom-livingroom in the middle. The whole thing was only about 10 ft x60 ft and was barely big enough to let people move around in let alone put furniture in it.

Rusted around the edges of every window, you prayed there was enough plastic in the county to cover all the windows in the winter to help stop the cold and wind from coming through. But it was the only thing her mom could afford after her great-grandmother passed away some years ago.

"Mom?" She yelled again, when she got to the end of the hall where it met the kitchen. It was then that she realized the trail of blood had gotten heavier. A knot of fear caused all of the neurons in her brain to start firing. *Oh my God, what happened?* Feeling sick, but not being able to quash the curiosity, she walked further.

Nothing but silence followed her. It was so quiet, she could hear the leaves rustle outside. A nice cool fall day had collected around the area. Sunday's were normally quiet, so it was no surprise that nobody or nothing was anywhere to be found.

All of a sudden she thought she heard a faint whimper. But it was so faint that she dismissed it as nothing more than the wind. But the closer she got to her mom and stepfather's bedroom, her stomach started to dance. *What the hell was going on?* She glanced around, nothing but silence. But she did notice that it had to be about 5pm because it was getting darker. Not dark enough where you couldn't see anything outside but the sun was no longer out so she knew it was getting close.

Then she saw the black leg with fur, sticking out of the bedroom. And all around it, blood. A big pool had made its way into the room, where the animal lain. *Oh God no! Not Spooky!*

She ran as fast as her legs would let her, into the bedroom and that's when she saw the carnage. Spooky lying on the floor next to the bed, his throat had been slit. Her eyes ventured upward to the bed and there on the bed, her stepfather's body lied motionless, covered in blood.

She tried but she couldn't make it stop. The bile came up from her stomach so fast that she never had a chance to make it to the door. Burning as it came up, the vomit shot out of her mouth like she was in a recreation of the Exorcist.

Then that she noticed her mother's favorite kitchen knife was sticking out of her stepfather's chest. Trying to gather herself, she looked around again and noticed blood was everywhere. Coming out of his nose, his eyes, his hands battered so bad that they had instantly bruised. Blood was even on the wall, dripping down like someone had popped a balloon that was filled with the best sanguine fluid ever. The window had a spider web crater in the center, like someone's head almost went through it. And in that center, there was black hair and lots of blood.

More bile came rushing up and out. *Get yourself out.* She thought. Mustering all of the strength she could, she made her legs move and staggered out of the bedroom. Trying to focus herself, she started to think of where the phone might be. *Where the hell is it?* Making herself look, she glanced around the living room.

There it is! On the end table untouched was the phone. She saw it, but could hardly get herself to move. Her legs so weak that she thought she was going to collapse, again. Willing herself to move, she slowly took one step at a time. Not wanting to look at anything, out of fear of getting sick again, she kept her eyes focused on the phone.

Picking it up, she was relieved when she heard the dial tone. Taking a deep breath, she picked up the cordless and dialed 911. In no time a dispatcher come on the line.

"911 what is your emergency?" the dispatcher said.

"Hello? Is anybody there?"

"I-I need help. There is blood everywhere. Oh my god. I don't know what happened!" she cried.

"Ok ma'am. Just calm down. You said…"

"Calm down? How can you tell me to calm down when there is nowhere that I can look without seeing blood. My stepfather is dead in his bed with a knife sticking out of his chest and my fucking dog's throat has been slit. I can't calm down!" she screamed.

"Ok hun. Take a deep breath and start by telling me how old you are." the dispatcher said.

"I'm 18. Please it doesn't matter how old I am. I am scared. Get someone here to help me! There is blood all over. And I can't find my mother!" she said.

"Alright, the police are on their way. Can you tell me anything else?"

"I don't know. I woke up and yelled for my mom and when she didn't answer me, I got up to look for her and that's when I noticed all of the blood." She said suppressing more bile.

"Ok. Do you have any idea who might have done this?" She started to sob so much that she couldn't control herself.

Why did this happen? Why is there blood all over? Oh God I'm just a kid, why did this have to happen? Did the neighbor's hear anything? Well why would they? They never hear anything that mattered. They never get involved when someone in is trouble. Even when the screaming got so loud your ears wouldn't stop ringing.

"Miss, are you still there? Did you know who might have done this to you and your stepfather?" the dispatcher said.

"Hurry! Help me. I think my mother just killed my stepfather, and tried to kill me too." she said.

Chapter 16

"Sheriff, we just got here ourselves and from what we can gather its one big blood bath. The blood trail starts in the kitchen and led us into the bedroom where Mr. Yeager's body was, along with the dog's body. I have Mr. Yeager's stepdaughter in the back of the cruiser. Her name is Cassie Damien. She is the one that called it in. She said that she woke up and found the mess after she couldn't find her mother. Sheriff, this is mess, this whole situation. Something isn't right. Yeager was beaten then stabbed and we also noticed an arrow sticking out of his abdomen. Whoever wanted this man dead, was bound and determined to make sure that he wouldn't find a way out."

"Deputy Sherman, make sure that this whole area is taped off, ok? I don't need any nosey neighbors getting too close to my crime scene, especially since CSU hasn't gotten here yet. I need you to take point on this because no telling where this whole thing is going to take me. But you damn well better make sure that if you come up with any new information that you call me first no matter what. Now how old is this Damien girl?"

"She says that she is 18. But with any kids, especially from around here, no telling if she is telling the truth or not."

"Are you assuming that all of the kids from a lower class income are bad?"

"No sheriff. I'm just saying......"

"Well next time think before you speak." *Where the hell did that come from?* "Well no matter, use kid gloves with this case. I don't need the damn media and newspaper junkies and photo happy sonovabitches camped out all around here and my front yard too. It's bad enough that two agents were blown up and the town is in a upheaval about that, this latest blood circus will push them all over the edge. I don't know what the hell is going on around here but until I find out, everybody will be working overtime until we catch the person or persons responsible."

"Yes sir. I am going to take Cassie to the station and talk to her and see if I can get anything out of her."

"Remember, take it easy on her. We are not bullies. Play nice until there is something that makes us think otherwise."

"Yes sir."

Sheriff Garcia walked into the trailer not knowing what to expect. The trailer was small so it didn't take long for him to look it over and see the mess. It also didn't take long for the enclosed space to fill with a putrid, smell of death.

Slowly walking to his left, the sheriff looked down the hall at the opposite end of the massacre. He found that even the bathroom had blood in it. The initial look through found a blood splatter pattern that looked like someone lost balance almost and tried to steady themselves against the wall. Returning his attention back into the hall and towards the little bedroom, the sheriff noticed that there was things busted, broken glass and holes in the walls all over the little trailer. *Something happened here.*

He's right. Something is wrong here. It's over kill. What the hell? Who would want him dead? Who hated him so bad? Sheriff Garcia kept thinking to himself as he walked the scene. He knew something wasn't right. He also knew that this wasn't going to be an easy case to deal with let alone solve. *Where was everybody? Why didn't anybody hear anything? Something's not right.*

Walking back down the hall and into the little living room, the sheriff noticed that the door hadn't been forced and none of the windows were broken. There were no indications of a robbery and besides the fact that there was more blood on the furniture, nothing made any sense.

The sheriff tried to recreate, what happened leading up to the blood bath but there were too many variables, so many unanswered questions and so much blood that it was hard to determine where to start.

Looking to the left yielded a broken down refrigerator and rusted out framed windows. Looking to the right was an old wooden style record player, a shot out window and so much blood that even Hitler would be shocked. Shards of glass were littered all over the little living room. *Is the shot out window an old thing or new?*

"Sheriff? Sheriff there is somebody on the phone for you outside." the deputy said.

"I will be right there."

"Yes sir."

Sheriff Garcia was still in shock and he couldn't believe that something like that happened right here; right in his own back yard. But little did he know that the shock would be deeper and closer than he imagined.

"I'm Sheriff Garcia. What can I do for you?"

"Sheriff let me start off by saying that I know you are an honorable man and that you will do what's right."

"Who did you say you were?"

"I didn't. I know what happened and I know that you don't have the resources to thoroughly solve this case. So just let me say this, it might be in your best interest to wrap it up quickly and call it a day."

"You're not suggesting that I bury this case are you? Because I don't know who you are, but I don't take to idle threats. You will not scare me and you will not intimidate me and you sure as hell will not tell me how to run *MY* investigation. So let me tell *you* this, if I ever hear from you again around town or if you ever show up in any crime scenes, you will regret it. Understand?"

The caller hung up and the sheriff went back to mumbling to himself.

"Sheriff, are you ok?"

"I don't know. But you can be sure that I will find out. I see CSU is here, so I am going to go back to my office and start on the paperwork. If you have any problems, call me. I don't like what's going here. I don't like it at all. Something's telling me that this is bigger than you and me combined. First, the explosion and the deaths of two agents in this town and now the death of a virtual unknown here in his own home and some guy just threatens me. Somebody I don't know. Something's telling me that everybody better be on the lookout and cover their own proverbial asses because this is far from over."

"Sir, you have no clue who that man was?"

"No I don't, but I intend to find out."

Sheriff Raymond Garcia, the man who has his whole department looking up to him, felt like he was brought to his knees by someone from hell. He didn't know what was going on or who was really calling the shots. All he knew was that whoever or whatever was behind this, was going to make it look like WWII all over again.

Chapter 17

"AJ, what the hell do you think you're doing, huh? I told you not to get too close to anybody. If you're not careful, the boss is going to want your fucking head on a silver platter!" The voice on the other end of the phone said.

"You know what? I don't care. This girl is the innocent bystander in all of this. And if that means my ass being hunted to protect everyone, then so be it."

"Your ass will be hunted alright. You can bet on it. The boss will not be happy with you. He will think you betrayed him and will make sure that he has your ass. You better watch it, that's all I can say."

"Yeah yeah. Don't worry about me. We have to make sure that Robert Yeager pays for what he has done. That man is without, the vilest, the most repulsive sonovabitch I have ever seen, and I have seen a lot of shit throughout my life. Tell the boss that I will deliver. But I will also make sure that the Damien girl stays alive too. I don't care who likes it or not."

"Well the only thing I can say is that I will make sure that you have a beautiful service."

"Well aren't you just the comedian? Don't worry about me. You just make sure that the boss knows that I am doing my job."

"Yes ma'am."

"Funny."

"Call me later if something comes up."

"I will. You know how to reach me."

"AJ?"

"Yeah." "Watch you're back."

"Yours too."

After the two hung up AJ couldn't help but wonder if she was doing the right thing. Fear was a good motivator. But betraying the boss would likely get you killed. AJ knew she had to do something; the people she associated with were not the typical Ozzie and Harriet types. Some of them were stone cold killers, thieves and degenerates; people who could walk through the most dangerous housing projects and not even blink.

"Hey what are you doing tonight? I miss you. You think maybe we can do something, anything?"

"I miss you too," he said, "I won't get out of here until at least 6pm and by the time I get home and take a shower and get dressed it will be at least 7pm. That doesn't give us much time for anything."

"Don't you worry about the time. Let me deal with that. You get home and take your shower and I will be at your place sooner than you expect. And wear that cologne I like."

"Oh? What did you have in mind?"

"Don't you worry about it, just get ready. I will probably be there before you. I can't wait to see you." AJ hung up.

AJ's life had always been a mystery to people. The only thing they knew was that she did have a social life but beyond that, they didn't know who she was dating or how long she had been seeing this mystery man. The only thing they did know was that he made her happy. And for those people she worked with, when AJ was happy, everybody was happy. When she was in a bad mood, they knew enough to be somewhere else.

Looking through the files she had on Shorty Santoro, she noticed it was missing a key piece of information, the low-down on Mufintano himself. Why? She wondered. Mufintano was the head of one of the biggest crime families on the East Coast. *Why wouldn't anything on Mufintano be in there?* She wondered. *Who the hell had access? Who could have buried this?*

Studying the file, AJ felt as if she was being watched. The hairs on the back of her neck began to dance. "Will you do me a favor? Do a drive by and watch my place. I don't like the feeling I am getting. No

I'm not staying home tonight. What does it matter where the hell I am going or what I am doing? Who the hell do you...you know what kiss my ass. I'm taking a shower and getting out of here. No. I have a life too you know. Shit I don't care if the boss doesn't like it. I will see you in the morning. Bye." She hung up.

"Look, I am not..." she began to said as she was picking up her cell again, "Oh hi. Yeah I am getting there. She is warming up to me. I don't like this. I don't like betraying her. She is a good kid. I don't think she did anything wrong. I told her that she needed to do something. Usually the first instincts are the correct ones. Yeah I know. Too close. Don't worry about it. She's just a kid right? Look, gotta go. Plans you know. Call me tomorrow. K bye."

You know I swear the man that invented the cell phone should be shot. "WHAT? Oh, it's you. What do you want?"

"Yeager's dead."

"What?!"

"Nobody knows anything other than he is dead in a bad way. I mean stabbed, shot and beat to death. Whoever wanted him dead, meant it, you know what I'm saying?"

"But who do they suspect?"

"Your girl's best friend."

"That's absurd. They stayed the night together."

"Actually, Cassie said that she woke up in her room with a bad headache and went to find her mother and when she walked towards the other end of the trailer, that's when she found the mess. Her stepfather and her dog, slaughtered."

"Holy shit."

"Any ideas, before this comes back and bites us in the ass?"

"Ah, no. Let me think about it and get back with you." The line went dead. *Oh my God.* AJ thought. Never did she think that Robert would be killed or at least not this soon. *Three different ways to die? What the hell is going on here? People are dropping like flies. Damn.*

AJ knew something wasn't right. She didn't know who she could trust or who she could turn to. All she did know was that she had to make a decision before it would be too late. Yeager was dead. Mufintano and his crew was in town. And this catastrophe was far from over.

AJ knew when she started with this whole debacle that it would be a touchy one. But she didn't realize that she find herself so drawn to certain people. She didn't know that she would feel like she would give her life for them. She didn't know that she would question her mere existence. The thought of the people she cared about getting hurt, scared AJ. The thought of her being scared, bothered AJ even more because she never thought she would be this scared in her life.

Chapter 18

Frankie called Mufintano's office reluctantly, hoping that the boss wouldn't answer the phone himself. Why? He wasn't even sure. He knew that Gaston was dead but trying to tell Mufintano that the job he sent him to do wasn't carried out by his own crew was going to be painful.

"Hey Carlos, what kind of mood is the boss in?"

"Well he just found out that Gaston is dead so he is happy about that, why?"

"Shit. He knows already? How the fuck did he find out?"

"I don't know. What the hell is your problem? You should be glad that it's over."

"See, that's the problem. Gaston was already dead and lying in his own pool of blood when I got there. All I could do was make it look good or better than it already was and get out."

"Shit. We don't need....yes boss....Frankie, let me call you back." Carlos hung up and turned to talk to Mufintano.

"Who was that on the phone?"

"Frankie. He said that he would be here shortly."

"Did he say if anybody seen him when he offed Gaston?"

"No he just said that he was on his way when you came in to talk to me."

"He's becoming a thorn in my side. Let me know when he gets here. And if you tip him off, you'll be next. Capiche`?"

"Yes boss."

Mufintano left the room and Carlos could breathe again. Even his own crew was afraid of him. He definitely had built up a reputation of being the most feared mob boss of all times. Gaston was dead and that should have been good enough. But Carlos knew that Mufintano wouldn't be happy because his crew didn't make the hit. Carlos knew he better make sure this didn't fall on to his shoulders and he didn't want to be around when Frankie told the boss that somebody else got to Gaston before they did.

He thought he hid the carbon crossbow well enough. He knew that it was all over and that Robert was dead. Nobody could have survived that shot. He saw Robert drop himself. Yeager was finally dead and wouldn't hurt anybody else. His family would be safe and so would anybody else that Robert could have come in contact with.

"Where are you?" the voice said.

"At work. Look I still have a lot shit to do, I will call you back as soon as I get the chance." and he hung up.

All of a sudden, he had a thought. *What if Robert didn't die? What if he was seen? What if the neighbors heard something?* His conscience was already messing with him. He didn't know what to do. *Wait a minute, just keep it to yourself and you will be fine. Nobody will know who killed him.*

Staring out the window in the office, he knew that he did the right thing. He knew that he saved his loved ones the pain of doing it themselves. Robert is dead and that's all that counts. But before he knew it, the phone rang. "Robert Yeager is dead."

"Who is this?"

"Don't worry. Just know that Robert is dead and I know who killed him. All I have to do is prove it."

"Sir, I don't know what you're talking about. What makes you think I know who you're talking about?"

"You know him. Everybody does." All of a sudden the line went dead.

What the hell was that all about? He thought to himself. Going back to work, he couldn't help but have the lingering thought of somebody knowing what he had done. Did the caller know him? Who was the caller? He began to wonder if he did the right thing, but who could have seen him? Who knew that he killed Robert Yeager? One thing was for certain, if he didn't keep his collective thoughts to himself, he might as well kiss his own life good bye.

"Get me Deputy Sherman on the line."

"Yes sheriff."

The sheriff couldn't stand idly by and do nothing. He knew that it had only been four hours since the discovery of Roberts' body. But not knowing anything was driving him insane. It seemed like a lifetime before the phone rang.

"Sheriff, we just escorted the body back to the M.E.s office. Dr. Prentice said she would call you when the tox screen is done and when she has something for you."

"Is CSU still at the scene?"

"Yes they are wrapping up. Sheriff I have a bad feeling about this whole thing. There are four different methods of death and one body. This town is in for one hell of wakeup call when it hits the papers and the local news."

"Yeah I know. But until then we have to keep this as quiet as possible. Do not talk to nobody unless it comes from me, understand?"

"Yes sir."

"And another thing, what did the M.E. say about which method could have killed him first?"

"Dr. Prentice didn't say. The only thing she did say was that it was going to take time before we know anything."

"Ok. Go talk to the neighbors, her best friend and get back with me as soon as you know something."

"Yes sir."

Sheriff Garcia didn't like not knowing anything. He hated to wait. But part of it might have been because this hit him more intimately than expected. He thought for a split second if maybe he should excuse himself from the case. Then he thought that there was no way he would let anybody handle his two loves. *I lost her once, I am not going to lose her again. Even if I had to hide her myself.*

"Yes director. Garcia made me lead in this investigation. I still think that there is more going on than he lets on. I get the feeling that Sheriff Garcia knows who might have killed Gaston. And if he doesn't he is playing stupid real good."

"Well we can't afford to go on your gut instinct right now. You might be right but who knows? Garcia might not know shit. So before we go off half-cocked and assume that we have this whole thing solved before the body cools, we need to be careful. You just do your job and let me worry about Garcia later. Remember, we are all on the same side here. Our job is to figure out this whole mess and close it up. Unless Sheriff Garcia crosses the line to the dark side, don't worry about him. Understand?"

"Yes sir."

After Agent Ritter walked out of the director's office, he couldn't help but think about Sheriff Garcia. *Something isn't right with him. Ray knows something damn it. Or at least he's hiding something. There is something about him that makes me believe that he knows more than he's letting on.* Eric mumbled to himself as he got in to his H2. *What the hell?* Eric turned the key but it wouldn't start. All it did was kept rolling over but it wouldn't fire. Agent Ritter flew out of his truck just in time to narrowly escape the same fate the two previous agents had succumbed to.

Chapter 19

Cassie Damien sat in a rickety old wooden chair in the sheriff's department waiting to talk to Sheriff Garcia. She was a scared little girl at that point that wanted her mother. She had no clue as to what was going, didn't know where her mother was at and her step-father was dead. She had no clue what to do or who to trust. She was all alone.

The sheriff's department was a small, fairly high tech run operation. Everybody looks out for each other and does not stand for any type of intimidation, even if the person delivering the intimation is known to kill first and ask questions later.

"Ms Damien? I am Sheriff Garcia. I hope that my staff has treated you fairly. Now why don't you follow me into my office so we can talk?"

"Yes sir." All Cassie could do is follow the sheriff and hold back the tears. She didn't know what she was about to face and she didn't know what to make of the sheriff. Maybe she was facing some heavy charges simply because she didn't know what happened. She wasn't even sure if she didn't do it.

Waving a hand at the chair across from him, Sheriff Garcia motioned for Cassie to sit down. "Please, sit down."

"Yes sir."

"Ms. Damien, its ok. You can call me Ray."

"Sir, what's going on? Why am I here? I didn't kill my stepfather I swear." Cassie said as she started to cry. One minute she was in her own bed, reading her homework and drinking her Gatorade and the next she knew she was waking up with a killer headache and facing a vicious scene. Cassie didn't have any recollection of anything else. All she did know was that Robert was dead and her mother was missing.

"Sheriff have you found my mother yet?"

"No we haven't. I have my best men out looking for her. Now I need to ask you a few questions, ok?"

"Yes sir."

"What can you tell me about your stepfather? And what kind of a person is he?"

"Well he's damn drunk and a pervert. I told my mom a long time ago when she first mentioned that she was going to get married to him, not to do it. She just ignored me. Said that the only reason I didn't like him was because he didn't ever spend any time with me."

"What makes you think that he is a pervert?"

"Because he tried to rape me, and mom wouldn't do shit about it. I tried to tell her what he was trying to do to me but she wouldn't listen. I was afraid to be alone with him. There has never been a lock on the bathroom door and she wouldn't let me put a lock on my bedroom door."

"You say that he drinks a lot?"

"No, I said that he is a drunk. He was constantly riding his bike and picking up bottles and cans and turning them in for beer or cigarettes. He never worked the whole time I had known him. And the one time he did get a job it didn't last long because he showed up at work drunk and he got fired. Sheriff, I didn't kill him but I'll be damned if I am going to say that I'm sorry he's dead. Whoever killed him did us all a favor."

"Cassie, have you ever seen him trying to do anything wrong to anybody else besides you?"

"No I haven't. But it wouldn't surprise me if he had. That man was sick. And something else, it always seemed like he was scared that somebody was after him. Robert was always talking shit when he was drinking about how he knew people were after him. That if I wasn't careful and if I didn't listen to him, he would have those people do to me what he did to some woman back almost 20 years ago in New Jersey."

"He said that?"

"Yes sir he did. I don't know what he did, I don't care. I just want you to find my mother."

"I promise we will find her. You said that he talked a lot when he was drinking?" "Yes. Sheriff, what's going on? I'm not a little kid. I just went through hell so I think I deserve some answers myself."

"Wow, you are your mothers' child."

"Excuse me?"

"Never mind. Cassie, I want you to stay here until we get a handle on what's going on, ok?"

"Am I under arrest?"

"No. But for your own safety, because we don't know what's going on, I would rather you stay here. Are you hungry? Would you like anything?"

"No. I just want to find out what the hell is going on."

"Somehow we will figure that out, I promise."

Sheriff Garcia got up and walked out of his office and closed the door. "Make sure she doesn't go anywhere." he said to the guard at the door.

"Yes sir."

He didn't know what to make of the whole situation. Ray didn't know if he should believe Cassie or not. Something was telling him that she was telling the truth and he knew who was behind Robert's death.

"Sheriff, you have a phone call. Line 1."

"Thanks. This Sheriff Garcia. What can I do for you?"

"You just lost another agent. Car bomb I think. If you don't back off of this investigation, I can guarantee that you and or anybody close to you will be next. Now, don't bother trying to find me. Just listen to me and everything will be just fine. If you don't, well then I hope you don't want any more children." The caller hung up and Sheriff Garcia became irate. "Sonovabitch! Tell me you know where the fuck this call just came from?"

"Sheriff, you never said to attempt to trace it." Desk Sergeant Harris said.

"You're kidding me right?"

"No sir."

"Damn it! Figure it out. Find out where that phone call came from. I don't care what you all have to do, or how much overtime occurs. Find that bastard and bring him to me!" Garcia stormed out. It has been a long time since Sheriff Garcia cared this deeply about anything. Everybody knew that this was personal at this point. But what they didn't know was how personal it really was.

Sheriff Garcia sat in his car, trying to breathe and bring his blood pressure back under control. He knew that he shouldn't let the caller take control of the situation, but it was hard considering the parties involved. The love of his life is gone, missing and his daughter might be a suspect to the murder of her stepfather. That would be enough make anybody a little cranky.

Going over his notes after his breathing returned to normal, he noticed that Cassie mentioned that she was reading, drinking and then woke up with a bad headache. That was enough for the sheriff to believe that Cassie had been telling the truth. Sheriff Garcia started his car and sped off to the one place where he could get any answer about his suspicions. He knew that it would be just a matter of time before the caller would return.

Chapter 20

"Mrs. Yeager?" The officer asked.

"Yes?"

"Ma'am, you need to come with us. It is for your own safety."

"My safety? What the hell is going on?"

"Just come with us and I will explain on the way to the sheriff department."

"Sheriff's department? Again? I'm not going anywhere unless you tell me what this is all about."

"Ma'am please, come with us and I promise we will make sure that you know everything and if you still have questions you can ask them to the sheriff. Please we need to go."

With that being said Jessica Yeager reluctantly got in to the police cruiser and prayed. Not knowing what was going on was the worst part of it all and it didn't help none that the cop wasn't going to tell her any more than he had to.

"I'm in your damn car now tell me what's going on." Jessica said as they sped away.

"Mrs. Yeager, when was the last time you were home?"

"I beg your pardon? Why is it any of your business?"

"Ma'am how was your relationship with your husband?"

"What the hell is going on? What do you mean was?"

"Mrs. Yeager, please just tell me when was the last time you were home?"

"Just this morning, when I left to go to work. Then after work I had some shopping to do. I left about 9am and then you burst into my life.

Now what the hell is going on? You either tell me or you won't get shit out of me until I find a lawyer."

The two officers looked at each other and then officer one started to talk again. "Mrs. Yeager, I hate to inform of this but your husband is dead." Both officers were waiting for any type of reaction from Jessica.

"What the hell are you talking about? I just talked to him this morning before I left my house. He was fine. My daughter was sleeping because she was complaining about not feeling good last night, so I didn't wake her when I left. Otherwise I would have taken her with me. And Robert was planning on going back to bed. He knew I was leaving. What did...what...who found...." Jessica kept talking and rambling until the reality hit her. She could tell by the looks on the officers' faces that they were not kidding.

"Oh dear God! How did he die? What happened?" Jessica wailed. The two officers were watching Jessica to see what kind of reaction she would give. To them it seemed genuine.

Jessica took a deep breath, "Why are you taking me to the sheriff department? I want to be with my daughter. Where is Cassie? Who found Robert?"

"That's the thing ma'am; your daughter is the one who found the body. And she is the one that called 911."

At that moment, Jessica Yeager lost all color. She couldn't believe that her daughter had to face whatever carnage was there. "Tell me that you have her somewhere safe?"

"Yes ma'am. She is with the sheriff right now and he is talking with her." The officer said as he was carefully watching her facial expressions. *If she's hiding anything, she is doing a damn good job of it.*

"We're almost there." Officer two stated as he carefully maneuvered the corner.

"What the hell is going on here? First you tell me that my husband is dead and then you tell me that my daughter is the one that called it in? What are you not telling me? Tell me now!"

"We will let Sheriff Garcia explain everything to you."

"You know what? I don't like this and I don't like you." Jessica yelled as she was helped out of the police cruiser. As the two officers walked in with Jessica Yeager, she took in the site outside the front doors.

She was just here 3 days ago when the federal car exploded. She felt it hard when she was thrown back. She saw the flames burning the two agents alive. She could hear their screams even though her ears were damaged from the explosion. Jessica knew that something wasn't right with the whole situation. And even now she wasn't sure what to think or who she could trust. Jessica Yeager was in a place where not even the strongest of men would want to be.

"Mrs. Yeager, please follow me." the deputy said as he lead her down a long hall adorned with pictures of officers past, some dating all the way back to what seem like the beginning of time. Some had captions above the photos that said 'In Memorial Of". "Mrs. Yeager will you please have a seat and I will tell Sheriff Garcia that you are here." the deputy said as he motioned for her to sit in a chair outside the sheriff's door.

"Sheriff, Mrs. Yeager is here outside your door when you're ready."
"Ok thank you."
"My mom is here!" Cassie exclaimed. "Why is my mom here? What have you guys done to her?"
"We haven't done anything to her Cassie. Please calm down and I assure you that she will be fine, as will you."
"Sheriff, what the hell is going on? Was it a full moon last night? First, the two dead agents. Now my step father? I'm scared sir."
"Your mom is outside my door, I swear. And if you let me I will talk to her and find out her side of the story."
"What story? Sheriff I'm not a baby, you can talk to me."
"Yeah this I know."
"Excuse me? What's that supposed to mean?"

"Never mind. I need you to tell me what you remember leading up to you finding your step-father. Anything you can remember will definitely be helpful."
"I don't remember anything. That's just it. I came home from school yesterday, grabbed my bottle of Gatorade out of the fridge and went to my room so I could do some homework. The next thing I remember it getting dark and it was really quiet in the house. I started to get up so I could go talk to my mom and when I tried to get up it felt like my

head was splitting in two and I felt really dizzy and my legs were really rubbery. I stumbled down the hall towards my mom's room and that's when I noticed all of the blood and ……….and I find out that it was the next day." Just about that time Cassie burst into tears and began shaking. Having to relive that whole terrible night just proved almost too much for her again.

"Cassie, honey, look at me. I won't let anything happen to you, I promise. But I need your help. I know that this is painful for you but in order to find out who killed your step-father we need to hear everything. Nothing is going to happen to you or your mother. No I don't think your mother had anything to do with Robert's death. But I do think that someone wanted to make sure that you couldn't identify them. Come on; let's go get your mom. You can talk to her for a few before I talk to her."

Sheriff Garcia opened the door to his office and there in front of him was a woman who would always hold his heart. If it wasn't for the fact that the human heart is inside the body, you could hear Sheriff Garcia's heart skip a beat when he looked at Jessica. And it made it all worse when he thought he lost her yesterday after the explosion and Mufintano's men taking her.

"Mrs. Yeager, would you please come in to my office so we can all talk?"

"Mom!" Cassie exclaimed as she thrust herself in to the waiting arms of her mother.

"Shhh honey its ok. I am fine but I have no clue as to what the hell is going on here. But I damn sure will make sure that we know before we leave here. Ray you better plan on telling me something or we're walking out of here right now." Jessica stated. But neither Cassie nor Sheriff Garcia could figure out which one was more confused. Jessica was trying to figure out why her mother called the sheriff by his first name and the sheriff was trying to figure out why Jessica did it front of Cassie.

"Mrs. Yeager, first let me start by saying……"

"You start? You always liked to be the first person talking didn't you?"

"Ma'am, please?"

"Ma'am? Why are you being so formal? Why are you being so cold?"

"Mom. What is your problem? Sheriff Garcia is trying to help us. He needs our help. Robert is dead and so is my dog. Now please let him talk!"

"Cassie, you don't know who you're talking about. This man is......"

"Mrs. Yeager, please let's just get through this and we can talk about history later, ok?" "History? Sheriff what are you talking about? Why don't you want my mom to.....oh my God. I know who you are now! History my ass. You're my father!"

Chapter 21

Daphne paced aimlessly while waiting for the phone to ring. She never thought that she would be so scared for someone that she didn't know that well. It didn't take long for her to figure out who everybody was and where this town was headed. Unfortunately for Daphne she was in a place that she felt that she couldn't get into. Becoming fast friends with the possible murder suspect who was also, come to find out her half-sister and also getting close with AJ, with whom she didn't know anything about.

Daphne knew that they were related but she didn't know the specifics of her birth right. She knew that she had a half-brother who it seemed as if he didn't care about anything except himself. But unbeknownst to Daphne, Butch cared more than she thought.

Muskegon was known for its hustle, bustle, and love of sports and for its beautiful shoreline. But hidden behind the shadows lurked a secret that was best left covered. If its citizens ever found out that one of its upstanding members of society was actually a narcissistic madman, they would change their locks and quit their jobs and hide their children.

Daphne knew that someone was watching her the other night. She knew that something wasn't right. But now she caught herself constantly looking over her shoulder. She couldn't go anywhere without catching herself checking every door and every window that she passed by.

Recently new to being a renter left her open to the possibility of not having the security of family members close by. Being alone also gives your mind time to play games with you and making you vulnerable to attacks of the psyche.

Trying to get ready for work, Daphne went about her business but she was a lot more tuned in to every sound in her apartment. She jumped as her phone rang.

"Hey what are you doing?"

"I'm getting ready for work. Who is this?"

"Someone you know better than you think. I know who killed Robert Yeager. Do you?" And then the caller hung up.

What the hell was that all about? She thought. *I don't know who he was or how the hell he got my phone number but I'll be damned if he's going to scare me. Sonovabitch. How the hell did he know that Robert was dead?*

"Butch? Did you just get a phone call from somebody telling you that Robert Yeager was dead?"

"Now why the hell would someone call me to tell me that? Do you really think that I would really care? And even if they did why would they call me? What do I have to do with anything? I'm just a mechanic. Now if you don't mind I have work to do." and he hung up.

Wow. Has everybody gone crazy? Alright one more time. "Hey do you have a minute? I would like to run something by you. Yeah sure. Ok meet me in fifteen minutes. Yeah I know where. Bye." With one last chance to help her brother and sister, Daphne got dressed, forgot about the phone call from that mysterious caller and left.

Driving west on I-96, Daphne noticed a black SUV staying close, too close for her liking. At one point, Daphne thought it might have been her imagination considering there was a lot of traffic on the roads but it didn't take long for her to change her mind and decided to call AJ.

"AJ, where are you?"

"I am home right now. Why what's up?"

"I don't know. Something isn't right, somebody is following me."

"Are you sure? Where are you?"

"I'm on I-96. I just left my apartment, heading back towards town and there is a black SUV following me. They have been on my ass for about two miles."

"Honey there are a lot of cars on the road and maybe you're just imagining things."

"I'm telling you that someone is following me and I am not imagining things."

"Ok. What are they doing? Where exactly are you on I-96?"

"Every time I change lanes, they move. Every time I speed up, they speed up. I know that there are two men in the vehicle because I can see them in my rear view mirror. Something's not right AJ, I'm telling you I am not being paranoid. I am almost to Muskegon where you would take the North bound exit."

"Alright. Keep going and watch them if you can. Can you make it to work? I will meet you there."

"I will try."

"Ok see you in a few."

Daphne kept her eye on the SUV behind her while still driving. She didn't like it, not knowing who was following her or what the hell was going on. She knew that the town was in an uproar about the recent events, but she still couldn't figure out what it had to do with her.

Turning north-bound Daphne noticed that the SUV kept with her and turned the same direction. Now she knew that she wasn't imagining things. Then all of a sudden they started to go around her and pulled up beside her. It was then that she noticed that there was another one behind her.

Come AJ answer the damn phone! Where the hell are you? "AJ there's two of them now! Damn it, what do they want? AJ what the hell is going on? I can't shake them, they are now beside and behind me there is two of them!"

"Just keep going honey. Have they tried to do anything to you?"

"No! I can't get rid of them. I can't move now. I can't change lanes. They have me boxed in. I'm scared."

"Like I said, just keep going. I am already at work waiting for you."

"I'm almost there. I'm going through Center Park right now but they are still with me."

"Are they being aggressive with you?"

"No. What kind of fucking question is that? They are just following me and I don't like it."

"Well I wouldn't worry too badly if they aren't doing anything other than following you."

"What the hell are you thinking? I have two complete idiots following me, to the point of not letting me move. And you're telling not to worry? Are you completely mad?"

"Honey, I'm just saying if they're not hurting you I wouldn't worry too bad. Maybe they're just messing with you. Can you identify any of them?"

"AJ? Are you.....what's going? Who are you?"

"Don't ask the question if you're not prepared to hear the answer."

"What the hell is that supposed to mean? Who are you? And don't tell me not shit about just a friend. I want the fucking truth AJ!"

"Daphne, I can't tell you that. It might be safer for you if you don't know. Just know this, that I will not let anybody hurt you."

"AJ, I don't know what you're into but when I see you I'm going to kick your ass. You got it?"

"You can try. See you soon." AJ laughed and hung up. Daphne didn't know what to make of that conversation. But she got the feeling that the people following her were not going to hurt her after all.

Pulling in to the parking lot of Rosie's Cafe, Daphne looked for AJ's car but didn't see it. "Ms. Alexander, please come with me."

"I don't fucking think so, not until you tell me why the hell you were following me and who the hell you are."

"Ms Alexander, I promise I will not attempt to harm you in anyway. We won't hurt you, promise."

"Kiss my ass!"

Just about the time that Daphne was going to put a fight with the suited stranger, her phone rang "Daphne, will you stop giving Tobias a hard time and get in the damn car?"

"AJ? Damn it you have to stop doing this to me. Where the hell are you? You promised me that you would be here when I got here."

"I had to make sure that I wasn't followed like you. Please just get in to his car and he will take you to where I'm at."

"AJ, you and me are about to have issues. You got it?"

"Yeah yeah, take a number and stand in line sister." and the line went dead.

God I hate it when she does that, Daphne said to herself.

"Fine. You damn well better make sure that I will see AJ or whatever her name is or you and I are going to have issues too. You got me?"

"Yes ma'am. Now if you will please get in we can leave before it's too late."

"Tobias?"

"Yes."

"What's going on? Too late for what? What the hell is all of the secrecy all of a sudden?"

"I can't tell you, but I can tell you that she is not what you expect. But we are one of the good guys, I promise."

"Promise? Don't promise things that you aren't ready to back up."

"Ms Alexander, I never do."

All Daphne could do was stare at Tobias while they were driving. She didn't like the fact that she didn't know what was going on and she didn't like the fact that something was telling her that she was being betrayed by what she thought was her friend.

Taryn wasn't sure that she thought she was doing the right thing. She didn't like lying to her friends. She was only doing her job. Back in Jersey, Taryn knew she didn't have to worry so much because she wasn't out of her element. She didn't like having to take orders from a mad man, let alone betray those who she had become close to her. There was only one person she has come to trust for some reason but she didn't quit understand why. All she knew was that the one person she trusted was in the same position as her.

Alone with the thought of trying to figure out what to do, Taryn called that one person she hated to think about. "Hey, it's me. I need a favor. I need you to check out something for me. I need you tell me if you can mix Methadone and Xanax? No you can't.......no. Don't worry about it. I know what I'm doing. Yes I know the boss wants answers, and he will get them when I'm damn good and ready. Yes I know who I am talking about. No I'm not crazy. I am just getting really pissed off with the fact that nothing is happening and soon the sheriff will know everything. Yeah whatever just make sure that the boss stays off my ass. Fine. *Boa Noite.*"Taryn slammed her cell shut and tossed it into the passenger seat. *Sonovabitch.* Taryn knew what she had to do and she dreaded it. For the last time she talked to him, she almost didn't make it back out alive.

Chapter 22

Deputy Sherman lay there, not moving. It seemed like the explosion shook the whole block. Nobody was around to see the carnage. Nobody seen what had happened to Deputy Sherman. By the time the rescue units got there, there was nothing left of the SUV. It was fully engulfed. The only thing left was the frame.

It took a while for the rescue units to find Deputy Sherman and by the time they did, he was unresponsive. They couldn't get a pulse on him or any response to pain stimuli. The paramedics worked furiously to try and save him. They shocked him three times before he came out of V-fib. But he was nowhere near away from deaths door.

The paramedics loaded Deputy Sherman into the waiting ambulance and they sped towards Lady Grace Hospital. None of them knew if he was going to make it or not. The lead paramedic called ahead to the hospital to inform them that there had been another car explosion and that this time a sheriff's deputy was involved. By the time they got there, it seemed like everybody from the ER was waiting outside the ambulance bay. Shortly after the arrival of the ambulance, half the police force walked in to the hospital.

In what seemed like forever, everybody waited, pacing. There wasn't enough space in the waiting room for everybody that turned out. In more than one way, Deputy Sherman had touched everybody's life since this whole mess started. But the one person that should be there wasn't. The only person who was able to get inside Deputy Sherman head and heart, wasn't there to help pull him out of his downward spiral death dance. Deputy Sherman didn't know that the other half of his heart was battling her own fight to stay alive.

"Is there anybody here for Deputy Sherman?" the doctor said.

"We all are doctor. How is our boy?" one of the cops asked.

"Well, right now it is too early to tell. They just stabilized him and he is off to surgery. We won't know anything for at least 24 hours."

"Doc, what are his chances? Will he make it?"

"Like I said, it's too early to tell. If he makes it through the night then he might have a fighting chance. Excuse me, I have to get back in there and check in on him. Who do I talk to for any changes in his status?"

"You talk to me." Sheriff Garcia said as he walked into the waiting room.

"Ok sheriff. Deputy Sherman is not out of the woods but he is alive. He's lucky he got out of his truck when he did. It was the power of the blast from the explosion that threw him back on to the concrete that put him in his current state. Like I told everybody else here, he is in surgery and the next 24 hours will tell. Now if you will excuse me I have to check on your deputy and my other patients," and Doctor Reese walked out of the room.

"What the hell happened here?"

"Sheriff, we don't know. We all got here after the fact. From what we were told, Deputy Sherman tried to start his truck at the office and the next thing we know witnesses are saying that there was an explosion and Sherman is laying on the ground not too far from his truck."

"We just talked to each other. When I left, Deputy Sherman was still in his truck on the phone. So I left because I had to meet with......."

"Me." Director Colbert stated. "Sheriff, what the hell is going here in your town? Do you have any clue as to what kind of man Mufintano is? Do you know that he has half of my department in his back pocket?"

"Do you have any fucking clue, *Director*, what it's like to be down here in the middle of this mess? All of us," Sheriff Garcia swept his arm to point to all of the cops stuffed in the waiting room as he came nose to nose with Director Colbert,

"We have been busting our collective asses to try and stop this mad man. So don't stand there and act like you know what the hell *you've* been going through because you don't know shit compared us." By now the good sheriff was beyond pissed. If it weren't for the fact that he was in room full of officers that were heavily armed he would have laid out Director Colbert right then and there.

By this time, every officer and agent in the room were standing and in a ready stance. None of them could tell who was going to make the first move. "Come on director. We are all on the same side. We all need to work together to find and stop this psycho. Now what do you know that I don't?" For the longest time nobody said anything and everybody wondered where they went from here.

"I came down here from Quantico, because I got a tip that another one of my agents had been killed, well almost. Look sheriff, I don't want to have a pissing match with you or anybody else. I want what's best for everybody involved. Now we need to figure out something fast. Or else Mufintano will reign supreme. And I'll be damned if I want that to happen."

"What do you mean another one of your agents? There has only been two that were killed, they were blown up right in front of my eyes."

"No. The intel I have tells me otherwise. Sheriff why do you think that I am here anyway?"

"I don't......you sonovabitch! You mean to tell me that my deputy is actually an agent?"

"I had no choice sheriff. I had to see who was who here."

"You think maybe we could play nice finally and you tell me the truth from now on? Or do I need to kick you out of the sandbox?" Director Colbert and Sheriff Garcia were still standing nose to nose again and every single cop in the room was wondering who was going to blink first. Sheriff Garcia took a deep breath.

"Director, how many more agents are you willing to give up to help?"

"Not sure. Contrary to what people think I have my bosses too just like everybody else does. I will get a hold of as many as I can but I can't guarantee when they will be here. So until that happens, what do you want me to do sheriff."

"Director, I think that the best thing for you to do right now is to go back to your office and put a fire under someone's ass. We need help like yesterday. Let me and these fine boys get to work. I will make sure that if anything changes in Agent Ritter's condition we will let you know. I am sure that someone is going to stay here and the rest of us are going to get to work." After much male posturing, Director Colbert left and went back to Virginia and Sheriff Garcia got everybody together and began to formulate a plan as to how bring down Mufintano.

"Sheriff, how exactly do you plan on bringing down a man like Mufintano?"

"I don't know but if it doesn't happen really soon, more people are going to suffer. We have to stop him. So who is going to stay here and play running back for the doctors? The rest of us can all meet at my office first thing tomorrow morning. Seven am."

In unison, they all agreed and slowly left one by one. Nobody really wanted to leave but they all wanted to make sure that Mufintano was stopped. Now that the FBI was fully involved, there should be no stopping the investigation.

Sheriff Garcia walked up to the nurse's station and insisted on talking to Agent Ritter's doctor. "Doctor Reese, I want you and your whole staff to leak information that Agent Ritter didn't make it and keep the truth under wraps. Nobody is to know that he is alive. I want you to change his name, everything. I will be assigning a couple of plain clothes cops, each shift, to watch him. If anything happens to my agent, I will hold you personally responsible. Understand?"

"Sheriff don't threaten me."

"Look, his safety is key to this whole thing. It would be better if our suspect were to believe that he did what he started out to do. Kill him. Please doctor, don't buck me on this one. And please make sure that if anybody asks any questions, they get directed to me."

"Yes sheriff. Just one thing, what do I do with his personal belongings?"

"Find a safe place for them and I will pick them up in the morning."

"You got it."

After the sheriff was done talking to the doctor, he began to wonder who would be next and if he could actually stop Michigan's Most Wanted.

Chapter 23

The newspaper headline read "Local man killed in his own home". No details were given, but that was enough to make the locals fear the worst and start talking incessantly, starting rumors and guessing who might have done it.

The media circus surrounding Robert's death was nothing short of astounding. It seemed like everybody became an instant expert on the history of the city, its citizens and especially the man that provoked such excitement in its people.

Robert Yeager was one person that few people knew much about. He kept to himself, even when he went out in public to go to the local fishing hole or liquor store. He didn't talk to hardly anybody, even when someone said hello in passing.

There were rumors about everything possible with respects to the whole family. Even some of the news reporters from both the paper and TV started camping out in front of the sheriff's department and the field across from the Yeager home. At first some people started wondering if the Extreme Home Makeover team was in the area. The news reporters weren't the only ones with their cameras flashing. The neighborhood kids and some adults had their digital cameras and cell phone cameras going. No telling where their pictures would show up. Sheriff Garcia's worst nightmare had come true.

Sheriff Garcia pulled up to the sheriff's department but could hardly get out of his squad car before getting mobbed by dozens of reporters all asking questions, cameras flashing. The only thing he allowed out of his mouth was "No comment."

"Sergeant, what the hell happened? I was gone for an hour and there was nobody out there. I get back and now I have everybody in the state outside my office. I want you to call somebody in to help with crowd control."

"Sir, I already did that but they said that they couldn't get here until morning."

"Morning! What the hell am I supposed to do until then? Damn it! I am going into my office and call the state attorney and tell him what's going on and tell him that I need help."

"They already called. They said that they needed to talk to you anyway. They were aware of the explosions and the deaths of the two agents. They also said that they were aware of Mufintano and his crew being here. They were already setting things up for more help; we just needed to be patient."

"Patient? How many more people have to die before they send in the Calvary?"

"Sir?"

"Never mind. Just let me know when the state attorney calls."

"Yes sir."

Sheriff Garcia reluctantly made his way into his office, knowing that he had to deal with the media circus but using paperwork as an excuse to not having to go back outside. Everything was running through his mind about Mufintano and his path of death and destruction, Robert Yeager and who he really wasn't, finding out that the love of his life and daughter, could be suspects in Robert's death, and the plethora of other usual suspects in the twisted game of who will live or die next.

Just then the phone rang pulling him out of his reverie, "Sheriff Garcia?"

"Yes."

"Do you know who is going to die next? I do." The caller quickly hung up.

What the hell is going on here? Garcia said to himself. The phone rang again, but this time it was someone he really didn't expect to hear from.

"What?!" the sheriff yelled into the receiver.

"Sheriff. I need to talk to you as soon as possible."

"Director, what is this about? I can appreciate the fact that you have concerns because of your deceased agents but I have one hell of a mess on my hands and I don't need some bureaucrat breathing down my neck telling me how to do my job."

"Sheriff Garcia, I usually don't put up with people like you and their attitude but I will cut you some slack considering the fact that you have a small town and limited resources. But the fact remains that you need my help. Two federal agents are dead in your county and you have one of the most dangerous men in your country, I don't know if you know but this is the big time sheriff."

"Your agents told me everything before they died. They told me about Mufintano and his crew. They told me that Robert Yeager really wasn't Robert Yeager, but that his real name is James Gaston. They even told me what he did and why Mufintano was here. So if you're done with your male posturing, I would like to get back to work. I will see you tomorrow. Good bye."

Smug bastard! Who does he think he is? Sheriff Garcia was pissed beyond imagine. The thought of somebody invading his town and telling him how to run it just set off Sheriff Garcia.

He normally wasn't an angry man all the time but that director got under his skin. Garcia didn't know if he should work with him or smack him around. Either case, Sheriff Garcia knew it didn't matter how angry he got at the man, his town needed him.

"Grand Central!" the sheriff barked answering the phone.

"Excuse me?"

"Sorry. Who is this?"

"Sheriff Garcia I need to talk to you, tonight. Meet at the west entrance of the old paper mill. Eight o'clock. Alone."

"Who is this?"

"Don't worry about who this is. Just know that the information I have could make your case and get the feds off your ass." With that, the caller was gone. *Is the circus in town?*

Sheriff Garcia looked at his watch and realized that it was almost 7:30 pm. *Sonvabitch.* Sheriff Garcia checked his gun to make sure that it was fully loaded and walked back out of his office. He knew that it was not good going into a scene without backup, but he didn't have any choice. All of his deputies were out chasing leads or investigating the scene or at the hospital.

Garcia didn't have to wait too long at the paper mill before a dark colored SUV was coming right towards him. An uneasy feeling began to form in the pit of his stomach. Something was telling him that he should leave while he had a chance. He could tell that there was only one person inside the vehicle yet it was too far away to say for sure.

It wasn't too long before he could make out the silhouette of the driver and notice that it was a female driving. *What the hell is going on here?* He thought to himself. Once the driver had pulled up next to Sheriff Garcia, he had a sense of deja` vu real bad. He knew that he had seen the driver before but he couldn't place it.

"Sheriff Garcia?"

"Yes." He said while unsnapping his gun.

"My name is AJ Kovac. I know that this is a bit unexpected but under the circumstances, I feel as if I didn't have a choice. I have sensitive information regarding Robert Yeager. Is there a place that we can go talk?"

Sheriff Garcia thought for a minute that this was a dream and that he would just wake up. But the more he thought about it, the more he knew that this was just the beginning. As much as he wanted to wake up any second, he knew that it would never happen.

"Look, I don't know you and as far as I am concerned we can do this here. Now."

"Sheriff, I can understand you're.........." Gun shots rang out and before they both knew it, bullets and broken glass went everywhere. It was then that the great sheriff knew that he could trust nobody.

Chapter 24

"Why should I listen to you? You can't even do your job right."

"What are you talking about? Yeager is dead and that's all that matters."

"He is not going to like this and you know it. Just because he's dead doesn't mean that you did your job."

"What the hell are you talking about it?"

"I'm talking about the fact that you left a mess and the police and the feds are going to find out who did it. Do you want to spend the rest of your life in prison?"

"Well the fact is, Yeager is dead and he had to pay for what he did. He hurt one too many people on his path to hell. It shouldn't matter how it was done, just the fact that it is done."

"I don't like it. Too many people know you, even if they are happy that Yeager is dead. Somebody is going to start spreading rumors and talking and the next thing you know the police and the feds are going to be looking for you. I can't protect you forever."

"I don't need you to protect me! I know what I did and I was willing to take that chance when it happened."

"Alright, I give up. I love you and I am going to worry about you. As long as the autopsy doesn't show anything we should be ok.

"Ok fine. Let's go. I love you too. If anything dramatic happens call me and I will come back home. Promise."

Both of them walked out of the restaurant with their coffees in hand and headed to the car. She set the navigator for a straight shot towards the Amtrak station and then set the cruise once she was on the expressway.

Nobody said anything for a few miles and then the next thing she knew, he was snoring. *Leave it to him to sleep. He could sleep through someone using an air compressor.* Her cell phone rang.

"Hello?"

"What are you doing right now?"

"I'm on the expressway headed towards the train station, why?"

"Are you ok? I mean you're a little snippy. I just wanted to take you to dinner so we can talk."

"Sorry. I just have been a little on edge ever since this whole thing with Yeager went down. I should be back in town around 6 pm. I will call you when I get home. I don't have to work tonight or tomorrow so if we can't do dinner tonight maybe we can do breakfast. Ok?"

"Sounds good. Hey, did you hear that the media is camped out outside the sheriff's department? I don't know how big this thing really is but whoever killed Yeager is going to be in for one hell of a rude awakening. It was also on the news that he was killed by more than one person. I hear that half of the town's folk are suspects. Could you believe it? Nothing ever happens in this damn town. There hasn't been a major crime in almost 50 years and now this. There is talk that even the mob is involved. Whoever did it should get a fricking medal for getting rid of that sick bastard. Anyway, let me know when you get back home and we can go from there."

"Well you know how people are, one little ripple on their pristine lawn and everybody becomes an expert on it. Anyway, yeah I will call you when I get home. Talk to you later."

"Alright, talk to you later." and both of them hung up. Not knowing what to make of the conversation, she kept driving towards the train station. The sound of the cell phone never even made him flinch. She was scared. She knew that this was going to happen. She knew that North Muskegon was going to be in an uproar when the story broke of Yeager's death, but she never imagined that half the county's news media would be camped outside the sheriff's department, let alone the mob was coming to town. *What the hell have I done?* She started doubting herself, even though she knew she did the right thing. *I had to protect them. He had to be stopped.*

She picked up her cell and proceeded to call the one person that she could always count on, "Hey it's me. He's leaving. Yeah, I know. See now you're just being nosey. No I'm not....will you just....whatever. Look, I'll be back in town tomorrow. Yes I know there are people looking for me. No he thinks I'm going out town on business. He doesn't suspect anything. Yes I know he is a good man. Don't you worry about me or him he loves us. Who told you that? They haven't even done an autopsy yet. How could anybody know how Yeager was killed? Drugs? What are you talking about? I thought he was shot? Damn! Ok. I will talk to you later. Gotta go." Hanging up her cell she began to wonder about how much information certain people knew.

"Hey wake up, we're here."

"Who was that on the phone?"

"Don't worry about it. You have a good, safe trip and I will see you in two weeks. Ok? I love you."

"I love you too. I will call you when I get there."

"You better. See you soon. Bye."

"Bye."

And with that, she watched him step on to the platform and then into the waiting train. There was nothing that she wouldn't do for him or for anybody that she loved or cared for. This was a close-knit community and also a nosey one. One where everybody knew everybody's business and it didn't take long for people to start talking. She also knew that it wouldn't take long before people started forming their own opinions on who really did it.

Chapter 25

"Sheriff? Dr Prentice is on the phone for you. She says that her autopsy is finished and she needs to talk to you about it."

"Ok thanks."

Sheriff Garcia dreaded the thought of going to see Dr Prentice, simply for the fact that he didn't think he was going to like the outcome. He knew that this whole scene was already getting out of hand, then having to add to the mix of sorting out the mess of the autopsy, not good. He knew that Robert's murder was not cut and dry. He kept thinking that someone close to him was probably going to end up being the suspect and that truly bothered him.

North Muskegon was becoming the latest battle ground in regards to crime. The latest victim in a long list of notorious people and their quest to having their fifteen minutes of fame. Children and adults alike were fair game. It seemed like whoever was behind this sick and twisted game, could be the next John Gotti or Charles Manson.

Sheriff Garcia proceeded to make the long walk from his office to his car and every time he got in to his car, he had to twinge when he turned the key. He prayed that he wasn't going to be next.

Driving towards the M.E's office, Sheriff Garcia had a thought. *Do I really want to know who is behind this? Do I really want to continue to be in charge of this case? It would be really easy to pass it over to the FBI like they want.* But the more he thought about it the more his pride got in the way. He was not going to let the FBI take control of his case.

"Sheriff Garcia?"

"Yes. Who is this?"

"You met with me the other night. I need to tell you something else and I can't do it over the phone."

"Ok. Same place, same time?" "Sure. But one thing."

"What?" "This time, make sure you're not being followed."

"I wasn't being followed the last time. What the hell are you talking about?"

"You *were* followed last time. Why do you think that I left?"

"I thought...." "You didn't think, that's the problem. Needless to say, you were being followed. I have something detrimental to your case. But just in case I don't make it, there is a key for a locker at the YMCA. You will get it in the mail if anything happens to me. Sheriff? Be careful this time." The caller hung up. *What the hell is going on with this damn town.* He said to himself.

Arriving at the M.E's office, Sheriff Garcia couldn't help but think about the phone call he just got. He knew who she was but he wasn't sure if he could trust her or should trust her for that matter. There was something about this whole situation that just rubbed him the wrong way.

"What do you have doc?"

"Well sheriff, I can tell you that any of the four methods used to kill Mr Yeager could have killed him on their own. First off..."

"What do you mean *four* methods? There was only a stabbing, shooting and bad beating. Three."

"Sorry sheriff, there was four. The fourth method was a bad drug overdose."

"Are you shitting me? Who the hell would......"

"Can I finish? I can tell you that he was beaten. Whoever was behind this was really pissed off. There was no stopping this person once they got started. They showed no remorse, they didn't care about anything. Mr. Yeager had to have done something; I mean really damning to deserve that kind of a beating. The beating alone would have killed him considering the amount of blood he lost."

"Yeah but doc, wouldn't he have lost a lot of blood anyway when he was shot and/or stabbed?"

"My dear sheriff. Don't take all of my glory. There is a method to my madness. I will tell you what happened in due time. Now please be patient."

"Fine. Just hurry up wouldya?" The sheriff said as he looked towards the door.

"Such an impatient man. When was the last time you went out sheriff? When was the last time that you got busy?" Jacqualine inquired with a smirk.

"What business is it of yours? Will you just....just tell me....." *Damn.* The good sheriff said. It had been a long time since any woman had gotten the best of him.

"Sorry sheriff. It's just too easy and you're too cute when you get flustered. Now where were we? Oh yeah. Blood loss. You're right sheriff, he would have lost some blood when he was shot or stabbed but one of those two was done post-mortem."

"You're really enjoying yourself aren't you?"

"Of course."

"Not funny."

"Ok ok. The crossbow shot he received to the stomach happened after his severe beating. He was beaten so badly that he suffered from severe internal bleeding. When I got him here, there was blood coming out of his nose, eyes and ears. There was a significant amount of swelling on the brain. Whatever your suspect used to beat him with also broke several ribs, cracked his skull and broke three bones in lower extremities. As I said, they were really pissed off."

"Doc, are you telling me that the beating alone would have killed him and nothing else?"

"Yes I am. I'm telling you that your man there didn't stand a chance." Sheriff Garcia was without words for the first time in a long time. He never thought that anybody in his town could be so hateful to the point of murdering anybody. Sheriff Garcia started to think about all of the people close to him. He wondered who would be willing to risk their life to wipe out somebody else's.

"Is that all doc?"

"Not by a long shot. Whoever shot him just shot him to make it look good. It wasn't a shot of any great distance. I would have to say that whoever beat him would have had to have put him in bed just to make it look like he was sleeping. Mr Yeager wasn't feeling anything when he was shot. There was already too much blood loss from the severe beating he took for that shot to make a difference."

"Holy shit." The sheriff said before covering his mouth in exasperation.

"Sorry honey but I'm not done. You said that when you found him there was a Bowie knife sticking out of his chest?"

"Yes why?" "Because, the knife in the chest was just there as a ruse to try to throw you off. The real killing wound was the slash across his throat. It was done with so much force that if whoever would have pulled forward; they would have ripped out his windpipe. Your suspect just stuck it in his chest to make it look good like I said."

"My God. Who the hell could have...."

"Sheriff, I hate to take you away from where you were just now but as I said, I'm not done."

"What are you talking about?"

"Mr Yeager was also poisoned. I found deadly doses of Methadone and Xanax. "

"Come one. You mean to tell me that someone else wanted him dead? You mean to tell me that there is more than one suspect in his murder?"

"Yes sheriff I am. Whoever beat him senseless was also the one who gave him the knife necklace. I know this because I found fingerprints on the body and prelim exam says that who's ever prints those are, are the same ones that I found on the knife. And then because of the time frame with the post-mortem poisoning and gun shot, it only makes sense that says that there are two others involved with that too. Sheriff, I don't know what's going on here but Mr Yeager here done pissed off the wrong people and good."

"So you mean to tell me that any one of those methods *really* would have killed him alone?"

"Yes sheriff."

"But I thought you said that the crossbow shot was just a gut shot?"

"It was but because of the distance and angle in which it happened, it hit a bone and a chip traveled upward and ended up ripping through and destroying the Inferior Vena Cava. And then of course with the bad beating he got, one of the broken ribs punctured his right lung. He stood no chance at all."

"Well shit. What a mess. I knew sooner or later this town was destined for great things. I just didn't know how much so. Thanks doctor, make sure that you cross your t's and dot your i's because I'll be damned if I let off these crazy people on a technicality. Call me if you find out anything more."

"I will. And sheriff?"

"Yeah?" "Be careful. There has already been enough loss of life of good men this week. We don't need anymore."

"I will. You just keep me informed." With that being said, Sheriff Garcia walked out of the morgue and began trying to piece together, all of the events that have transpired.

Holy shit! He thought to himself.

Getting into his cruiser Sheriff Garcia plugged a couple of names in to his car computer. He wondered how much worse this would get. He never imagined that one man could create so much chaos. While Sheriff Garcia waited for the computer to stop its searching, he began writing his notes. Then a fear reached in and grabbed a hold of his heart; who else that he cared for will be next.

Chapter 26

Nineteen Years Ago

Cecilia's heart was taken wholly by Anthony. She loved him and he loved her. And even though she knew that all good things come to an end she also knew that as long as she had Anthony, anything in her life was going to be far from boring.

Anthony was a young up and coming business man who prided himself on making sure that everybody knew that he was boss. It started early in his life when he would watch movies featuring all of the old mobsters. He wasn't sure who he liked better, Al Capone or the Gambino family. Mufintano tried to go straight more than once but never could quite make right.

Anthony had someone working for him that he thought would never cross him but before long he found out that he was wrong. James Gaston worked for Anthony Mufintano as a driver and basic errand boy. It didn't take long before he found out that he had better kept an eye on him simply because he didn't like how James would eye Cecilia.

Anthony brought James on because he once saved Cecilia's life when they were first married. Cecilia and Anthony were having lunch one day in a nice café in New York when all of a sudden a man with a gun came in and proceeded to rob the place. The man put a gun to Cecilia's head and ordered the cashier to take out all of his money or he was going to shoot her. For some reason unbeknown to Anthony, a total stranger grabbed the gun and wrestled the guy to the ground and held him at gun point until the police arrived. The stranger couldn't have been no more than twenty one years old.

Anthony wanted to thank the stranger so he ordered Frankie Cicero to track down the guy. It took a little doing but he found him. It was hard for Anthony to believe that the kid was so young and that he would risk his own life for a stranger. That in itself proved to Anthony that he was someone of worth, or so he thought.

James Gaston didn't know what to think of Anthony Mufintano. He knew who he was. He knew that Mufintano was not in the friend business, but yet he knew that he was on his own and had to do something. He was close to living in a box on the street, so he thought 'What the hell'. He never expected to fall in love with Mufintano's wife. But by then it was too late he was invested in to something that he really didn't want but had no choice. Gaston was caught between love for a woman he knew he could never have and keeping himself alive.

Gaston kept to himself and did what he was told. He kept himself alive for some time, did nothing stupid and made eye contact when the boss spoke. This went on for a few years until he couldn't help himself. One night late while in his room at Mufintano's mansion, he spied Cecilia going into the shower. She didn't know that she hadn't locked the door. Gaston seen it all, full frontal and he couldn't help himself he started to get aroused. He knew there was a reason why he loved her. Surprisingly she didn't scream, she just slammed the door shut and then locked it. That was the beginning of the end for Cecilia. She never saw it coming.

Shortly after the shower incident, Gaston kept coming up with excuses to spend more time with Cecilia. At first Anthony didn't think too much about it but after a while he ordered Frankie to start watching him. Mufintano would find more for Gaston to do so he wouldn't be so close to Cecilia. He was becoming more and more suspicious about Gaston.

One day Cecilia told Anthony that she was going in to town to get a few things for the big dinner they were throwing. She told him that she had to stop at the bank first and then she would be home shortly afterward. Cecilia Mufintano never made it home. They told Anthony that it was a botched bank robbery but he didn't buy it. He knew better.

After the funeral, Mufintano was sitting in his room trying to come to terms with the fact that his beloved was dead. He laid his head down on Cecilia's pillow and noticed that there was something hard underneath.

Anthony reached for the object and realized that Cecilia kept a diary. Not sure if he wanted to open it, he just sat there staring at the cover.

All it took was for Anthony to think about life without Cecilia and having to raise a child alone and tough guy extraordinaire was hit with the full strength of his emotions. The tears didn't stop for a long time, but once they did, he looked back down to the diary his beloved kept and found the courage to open it.

Anthony skimmed across the pages and didn't see anything really impressive and almost gave up on reading it. It wasn't until he came to the last page that something stopped him in his tracks. It was a specific name that jumped off the page and made him pay attention. 'Dear Diary: Gaston seen me as I got in to the shower today. I shut and locked the door to the bathroom. I haven't had any more issues with him but I don't know he is just starting to creep me out more. I don't want to worry Anthony because he has enough on his plate right now. I just think that I will just talk to Anthony soon about maybe him getting rid of James. We can start driving our own cars or he can hire someone else. I know that James has been loyal to Anthony but something off here. I will talk to him after the dinner party on Friday. I love Anthony so much I just don't want to bother him. More to come.'

Instantly Anthony Mufintano was pissed beyond all he has ever known. He was seeing red. It was at that point that he knew Gaston wouldn't live long. He knew that Gaston had something to do with Cecilia's death. He could feel it deep inside his soul. But he had to be careful; he didn't want his daughter to sense anything wrong.

It took Mufintano a while to plan out what he wanted to do with him and he wouldn't allow any of his men to carry out the hit. This one was personal. Mufintano wanted to do this one himself. It took him about a month to get everything together. He didn't let Gaston know that he knew anything. He wanted to keep him close, so he kept him on as a driver. As the old cliché goes, keep your friends close and your enemies closer.

When the time came, Gaston was long gone. He just up and left one day without warning. He left in the middle of the night while everybody was sleeping. He left everything in his room save for the clothes on his back and fled East Rutherford.

Things seemed to have settled down a good numbers of years later. Gaston found new work and Mufintano went about his business. Gaston never did stop looking over his shoulder. The stupid thing was he didn't go far enough away because he started watching someone he had never met before. A beautiful young woman that he thought that had captured his heart. He had a decent job, an apartment and was finally making something of himself. Gaston thought that he could get her to fall for him.

He frequented a little cafe almost every day for his favorite latte. The problem was that he didn't realize at the time but the woman that worked the cafe, was owned by her father. As the story goes that man had lost his wife years ago in a botched bank robbery.

Chapter 27

"AJ I need to know something. I need you to tell me who you really are?"

"I can't tell; you know that. Just know I am on your side, and I would never let anything happen to your sisters."

"But who do you......"

"Shhh, don't worry yourself about that." AJ said as she continued to slowly move her hands up and down his firm ribcage.

This was a disaster waiting to happen. AJ thought to herself but she couldn't help it. Not only did she want information out of Butch but she could feel herself falling for him. She was beginning to feel as if she was betraying him. *This was not supposed to happen.*

"Are you ok?" he asked "You seem a little distracted."

"I'm fine. I need to go. I have a meeting in a couple of hours and I can't miss it."

"Will you be back tonight?"

"I don't know. It depends on how my meeting goes." AJ said as she started to get up.

Butch didn't want to let her go. He loved the feeling of her snuggling up next to him. Never in a million years had he imagined himself liking someone as mysterious as AJ. Butch was the type of person who had to be in control. He had to be the one that knew where everything was going on. But when he ran into AJ at his sister's place of work, he couldn't keep his eyes off her. She was beautiful, vivacious and full of life. Not to mention that she wasn't afraid of anybody or anything.

"Don't leave yet. You still have a little bit of time." Butch said with a sly smile as he put one muscled leg on top of AJ's leg trapping her so she couldn't move. Without warning, he kissed her hard with so much passion that she couldn't think. She let herself go. Giving into the burning feeling she had whenever he was close to her. She kissed him back. Without thinking they both began their favorite pastime.

"I really have to go this time honey. I can't be late for this meeting. Do not follow me into the shower either, ok?" She smiled.

"You know I hate it when I have to listen to you." he frowned.

"Yeah I know but you love me for it anyway."

AJ jumped in to the shower and quickly washed her hair and her body. She hated to shower after sex with him because to her it was almost like losing him. Thoughts of them together swarm in her head, but then she came back down to Earth. She knew that it wouldn't work between them, it couldn't. AJ had fallen in love with the one person that she couldn't have. She loved the feeling he gave her every time she was around him. She loved the butterflies in the pit of her stomach. She loved him. *Damn it.* She cursed. Why did he have to make her take that assignment. Did he know what would happen? *Bastard.*

Getting out of the shower, AJ had a light bulb go off in her head. *No that it wouldn't work. The program gets people out of the hell that they are in and makes them disappear. Son of a bitch. Why me? Is this some kind of punishment for not helping my family when they needed me?* AJ went back to drying off. Just then Butch came in to the bathroom and stared at her.

"What?" she asked.

"Nothing." he said the kind of smile that someone got when they were totally blissed out.

"Are you ok Butch? You look a little peaked?"

"You're beautiful, you know that?"

"Butch sit down. You look as if you're going to pass out."

Butch sat down on the toilet seat and stared. All he could was think about her. He wondered how he gotten so lucky, and knew he didn't deserve her. He had been such a bastard to the people around him that he didn't think that anybody could or would love him back.

"I love you." he whispered so low that even he wasn't sure if he said it.

"What was that honey? I didn't hear you."

He smiled, "Nothing. I have to get back to the garage before the sheriff has my ass on a silver platter.

"Well we wouldn't want that considering it is such a nice ass!"

"Funny."

"Look, I don't want you worrying about anything, ok?"

"I don't know who you really are but there is something iffy about you and this whole situation. I find myself being drawn to you. How do you know about my sisters anyway? I never spoke about them. Hell I just met them recently."

"I have to go. Like I said I can't miss my meeting. Tell you what, I will call you when I am done if it's not too late." AJ got up, gave Butch a long deep kiss and left.

AJ felt sad as she got into her car. It almost felt like she wouldn't see him again. She didn't know how this whole scenario was going to play out or who was going to be alive in the end. She hoped that Butch wasn't going to get too close and get hurt. It would kill her if anything happened to him. But what she didn't know was that Butch isn't quite the nice guy that she had fallen for.

Driving to the old paper mill again, AJ began to get the oddest feeling almost as if she were being followed. Glancing at the rear view mirror, she couldn't see much considering it was dark and late but she still felt as if someone was behind her. AJ felt her side to make that her Glock was where it should be, readjusted her seat belt and kept driving.

Pulling in to the west side of the building she had an eerie feeling, yet nobody was watching, save for a couple of owls. Carefully AJ got out of her car and stood by the door long enough to check to see if the clip in the Glock was full. She put the gun back in its holster and but didn't snap it and then sat down to wait.

From the west came a set of headlights, but one block from the edge of the property they ceased to exist. AJ waited to see what would happen next. All of a sudden a car pulled up next to her, driver side doors almost touching each other.

With her right hand on the Glock, she watched Sheriff Garcia turn the car off and then turn to her.

"So what is this pressing urgent information you wanted to talk to me about this time AJ?"

"Sheriff Garcia, I know you know who is in your town, and that he is a dangerous man. But I need to know how much do you know about him?"

"I don't know you and I'm not sure what side you're on. So why should I just voluntarily give out information that could get more people killed?"

"Smart man. I heard about you and your cavalier ways. But nonetheless, your town has become a battle zone. And unless you want to start stacking the dead bodies up like cord wood, I suggest that you start trusting someone."

"What makes you think that I am going to start trusting someone that I just met, let alone someone who can't tell what side they are on. So until you make up your mind, you might want to go back to square one and rethink your priorities."

"Sheriff, get in to my car so we can talk about this more."

"Why? Huh? Why should I get into someone's vehicle without so much as a hint of what's to come?"

"Sheriff, please get in."

"Are you afraid of the dark AJ?"

"You're an arrogant bastard aren't you?"

"Yeah I have heard that more than once in my life. And for the record, I don't trust you."

"Fine, whatever, just get in the damn car so we can talk."

Sheriff Garcia got out of his unmarked cruiser, locked the doors and started to walk around the front of AJ's car. Just about the time that the sheriff put his right hand on the door handle of AJ's car, shots rang out and one narrowly missed the good sheriff's head.

"What the hell?" Garcia screamed as he dove into AJ's car.

"Get in!" AJ screamed as she returned fire to cover for the sheriff. AJ tromped on the gas and spat gravel all over Garcia's car. Not looking back, she kept the speed full bore, splitting open a twelve foot wire gate in the process. AJ tried to think straight while Ray returned fire into nowhere. When they thought that they were out of danger, it was only then did either of them speak.

"You were followed!" AJ yelled.

"Me? What makes you think that it wasn't meant for you? Or that you set me up? Huh? You were the one that suggested meeting here *again*. It was your idea to meet at this specific spot at a specific time. So don't fucking tell me that I was followed." About that time Sheriff Garcia put his gun to AJ's temple and told her to drive him to his office and that she was under arrest.

"You don't have the authority sheriff. You can't arrest me."

"Bullshit." he said as he cocked his gun.

All AJ could do was laugh at Sheriff Garcia. It's not like she had never had a gun put to her head before. It was nothing to her. She kept driving and talking.

"Check it out. Check out my background. You can't touch me. I'll go along with your request but when we get to where we're going, you will be the one to answer to someone that you won't like."

"Just drive and shut up."

"What's the matter sheriff? You think that you're losing control of your precious city? Or could it be that you don't like not knowing all the answers. There are a few things you don't know but you're about to find out."

"Just drive. I know who you are. I know that you kick it with Mufintano and his crew and that that shot back there was probably directed at me, to shut me up so he could finish what he started."

"Nice story *Ray*. There's just one thing wrong with it. I don't know who or what was back there. I have no clue as to who was shooting at us or who it was directed at. So keep telling yourself that and maybe one day you could be right."

"If you're not who you say you are, then tell me who the hell you are!"

"I can't. I'm sorry."

Garcia tightened his grip on the Glock, "Well then I guess you get free room and board for a while."

"Sheriff, listen to me. You don't know what you doing here. I am not the bad guy, contrary to what you might think right now."

"Then tell me what I'm thinking, huh."

"You think that I work for Mufintano. You think that I had something to do with Robert Yeager's death and you think that any given time, you could be next. But you're wrong. Well on a couple of those points anyway."

"What's that supposed to mean?"

"Damn it sheriff! I'm a federal agent assigned to his case. And I am also investigating the deaths of my two agents outside your office door!"

Neither of them said anything. All they could do was ride in silence. After a few minutes, which seemed like hours, Sheriff Garcia dropped his gun. He didn't apologize but he dropped it none the less. The rest of the ride was eerie, almost like they had come back from a funeral. Neither AJ nor Garcia knew what to make of the whole situation. But they had one common silent thought, they each were about the only ones who could be trusted.

Chapter 28

"AJ. I know you told me that if anything happened to you there was something in a locker somewhere. But you got to tell me now. I, we, can't afford to hold off on anything. There are too many people closing in on this town. Hoping to use it as their own private dumping ground. Not to mention I have the director of the FBI breathing down my neck. If you are what you say you are, you have to trust me with this information."

"Sheriff. I *am* an agent. And I do trust you but that information was only supposed to be brought out in the case of an emergency."

"AJ. You don't think that this isn't a damn emergency?"

"Don't do that. Don't use guilt on me. I didn't have to tell you about it to begin with."

"I realize that and I thank you, but I have to do something. Why don't you work with me on this? You would know where the file is at all times and you can also keep an eye on me for your superiors."

"Director Colbert *IS* my superior or have you forgotten?"

"I know that. But damn it...."

"If I do this now and the director finds out, it will be my ass and I can guarantee that you will be going down with me on this."

"Fine by me." Both of them knew that if that file with all that information in got in to the wrong hands, both of them could die. Sheriff Garcia and Agent Kovac were both well of into a life that neither of them wanted.

"Sheriff. Is your office secure?"

"Yes. I had it swept myself. Why?"

"Forgive me if I don't believe you but I would feel better going somewhere where I know I can't be heard."

"Well then where the hell do you plan on going? You need to tell me and I don't care where we have to go but you need to tell me now."

"I know the perfect place. Meet me at old railroad tracks. You know the ones that were turned in to a bike trail. A lot of people go there to go fishing by the library. Meet there in a half hour."

"Alright, fine. But if you don't show up or if this is some kind of set up, I will see you in hell. Understand?" "Yes sir."

Both Agent Kovac and Sheriff Garcia went their separate ways discreetly. Not knowing if the other one was telling the truth. Not knowing if they should trust each other. But both knew there was a level of uncertainty and a morbid sense of curiosity drove them to meet at the agreed upon destination. The one thing that Agent Kovac didn't know was that the sheriff was already in the process of having her checked out. He was just waiting for the call back from Virginia.

Sheriff Garcia arrived first. He wanted to make sure that he could check out the area to making sure he wasn't being set up. This fall day was quiet; leaves rustling, not a soul in sight and an eerie feeling permeating the area.

"Sheriff."

"AJ."

"Now what? I'm here and hopefully alone. Now tell me what you wouldn't or couldn't tell me in my office."

"The locker at the Y contains information on Shorty Santoro, Anthony Mufintano and everybody else involved in his family. But the bulk of the intel in that file is about Santoro."

"And you couldn't tell me that in my office? Why?"

"Because there are people around you that I don't trust and I would rather err on the side of caution thank you very much."

"Who? Who in my department is dirty?"

"I never said they were dirty sheriff. I just said that I don't trust people."

"Well then tell me why you don't trust them."

"Too many things just don't add up."

"Bullshit. My department is clean."

"Ok then tell me one thing; why at our first attempt at meeting you didn't stay? Or our second meeting you were shot at?"

"How do I know that all of that might have been directed at you?"

"I'm a fucking agent sheriff!"

"My point exactly!"

"Look sheriff. I'm not going to get in to a pissing match with you. Neither one of us trust each other. We are both here now. What do we need to do to stop this?"

"My question to you AJ, is who is your informant?"

"How did you............."

"You're not the only one who has connections. Now answer my question."

"I have an informant inside Munfintano's camp."

"Does not answer my damn question. Now tell me or I'm outta here and so are you."

"Sheriff don't do this."

"Why not huh? I thought we were both on the same side?"

"That is not fair."

"Tell me or say good-bye."

"You're a bastard you know that?"

"Yeah I have heard that a few times. Spill."

"Damn it. My informant is one of Mufintano's so called soldiers, so to speak. She works at Rosie's Cafe. She has decided to turn on him. She has been gathering information on Mufintano for the past two years. We both had decided that it would be better to stay inside so he wouldn't get suspicious."

"Where is she now?"

"Safe. Waiting for me."

"It's Taryn isn't it?"

"Yes. And sheriff you have to promise me that she will remain anonymous. I will not allow that monster to kill her like he has so many others." "I will do what I can but so much shit has happened already that it is almost impossible to know who or what is what. Is she the one that poisoned Gaston?"

"No."

"Are you sure? Because I got information that says otherwise. Someone called in to the local pharmacy asking about the adverse reactions with Methadone and Xanax. Those are the exact two same drugs that would have killed Gaston had he not been beaten to death."

"Do you know for sure that it was her that called it in?"

"Actually I do. We have already traced her cell phone number. And simply put two and two together."

"Sheriff, she didn't kill Gaston."

"You don't know that for sure do you?"

"What good would it do her by killing Gaston?

"I don't know you tell me."

"Sheriff you can't be serious? There is no connection between her and Gaston. Hell there is more evidence with Daphne and the others than Taryn."

"Now why the hell would you even mention Daphne? What do you think she has to do with it?"

"Sheriff, you don't know anything do you?"

"Why don't you enlighten me?"

"Daphne's mother was attacked years ago and we have it linked to Gaston. After Daphne went off to college she decided to do some digging about her mother's death on her own. During this time she earned her degree in criminal justice, was recruited by the local police because of her skills and was asked to do some undercover work."

"How fucking many spooks are in my town? *Sonovabitch*."

"There is only three; two FBI and one undercover cop."

"You can't be serious? I thought it was bad enough knowing you were here along with Agent Ritter. Now you're telling me that Daphne is working my case too?"

"Yes and no. Daphne isn't working through your department, she is an undercover cop for the state police."

"Oh that's just fucking perfect. It's nice to know that everybody can get along."

"Sheriff. Like you, none of us were sure who could be trusted. Honestly, I don't think she even knows that we know who she is, and we have been watching her for quite a while."

"Do you trust her?"

"We have come to believe that there is no reason why you can't believe or trust her."

"I guess that's as close to a yes as I am going to get. So what do we do now?"

"We stop this once and for all."

"Yeah but how? That's the question. This whole thing is one big fucking nightmare started by a man who couldn't keep it in his pants."

"I like how you think sheriff. We need to get together with Agent Ritter and ask him a few questions about what he might have found before he got blown up."

"Should I trust him?"

"There should be no reason why you can't him either. And how is he doing anyway?"

"Alive for now. He's lucky if he walks out of here simply because I hate being lied to. He had already told me about his undercover assignment, but if either of you lie to me again, I kill you myself."

"I already said sorry. What the hell more do you want?"

"See, now is not the time to be cute."

"Sorry."

"Hey one more question. Could Taryn be the one that has been making all of these calls to everybody telling us shit about Gaston?"

"If she is, she is doing it of her own volition."

"I was afraid of that."

"Ok, tomorrow we should go to the hospital to see Eric. Is there still an uniformed officer posted outside his door?"

"How the hell do you know about the guard?"

"Because I tried to go visit him the other night and they wouldn't let me in."

"That would explain a lot."

"Excuse me?"

"Never mind. Tomorrow meet me at the nurse's station outside his door. Nine am."

"You got it. Sheriff watch your ass."

"You too. No more lies AJ. If something happens, you damn well better tell me."

"I will. I promise."

After that long meeting of the minds they parted with a better understanding of who was who and what was going on. Sheriff Garcia didn't like being lied to but part of him understood why they felt like they had no choice. Only thing is, the number of people left that he could trust was dwindling.

Chapter 29

"Dad, where are you going? I thought that you didn't have to work today? I was hoping that maybe Cassie could come over and we could take her with us when we went camping."

"Brandie, I told you I'm only working half a day or so don't worry about it. Cassie can come with us if she wants, but you better go ask if she still wants to go. I want to leave right away when I get back. Your mother already has all our stuff packed for the trip. So do what you have to do and get ready. Ok?"

"Ok daddy. Have a good day at work."

With that, Jamie walked out the door, got in to his car and left for work. He knew that if anybody found out what he had done, he could never see his family again. That thought scared the hell out him, his family meant everything. What he didn't know was that his family was already being watched.

"Mom, dad just left. I am going to call and see if Cassie wants to go camping with us. I just hope that Mrs. Yeager will let her."

"Ok honey, you be careful and I will see you when I get home." Terri said as they hung up.

"Sheriff Garcia? Can I talk to Cassie? I know that she is there with Mrs. Yeager. Wait, do you think it would be ok for her to go camping with us?"

"Well I guess but you need to tell me exactly where you and your family are going camping so I can make sure that there is someone watching out for you, ok?"

"Ok, I will. But you make sure that she knows that I called, we will pick her up at your office around 6pm."

"Ok Brandie. I will make sure that she knows. I am sure that she will be looking forward to it, considering she needs a break anyway."

Sheriff Garcia hung up and proceeded to finish his conversation with AJ.

"Ok now where were we? Oh yeah. You were about to tell me about last night and who the hell you really are or I am going to throw your ass in to a 6x9 cell."

"You really don't trust me? I thought we settled this already?As I said I am a federal agent working undercover. Nobody knows I am here and nobody could ever find out or it could get worse for both us. Mufintano is one bad sonvabitch as you have already found out. He and his crew have come to town because of James Gaston a.k.a. Robert Yeager. I know that's why the two previous agents were here to talk to you."

"Yeah I know all of that already. Tell me something I don't already know. Or you're outta here."

"Well did you know the real reason Gaston was in the program?"

"No. Why don't you enlighten me?"

"Gaston was originally placed in the program because he had Mufintano's wife Cecilia killed in a bank robbery."

"Bullshit. You and I both know that wrong place wrong time shit happens all the time."

"Yes, you're right, but, one of the men involved made sure that he targeted her, specifically. Gaston told this guy the pattern that Cecilia Mufintano had in regards to what she did regularly like getting her hair done, grocery shopping and going to the bank for her husband. So they knew that she was going to be at that specific bank at the right time."

"Shit. Are you sure?"

"Yes we are. So when he left town and Mufintano's employment, Mufintano made sure that he knew where he was at all times. When we got wind of the hit put on Gaston, we offered him protection in exchange for his testimony against Mufintano. But before we knew it, Gaston was gone."

"Is that all?"

"No." She said with a chuckle.

"Before we could find Gaston, his name surfaced again. Except this time we heard that he had killed Mufintano's daughter Theresa. Only Gaston didn't know who she was. He didn't know that he killed his former boss's daughter. He has also been on our watch list for multiple unexplained rape cases in the Fort Lee/Hackensack area."

"Son of a bitch. *He's* the one."

"Excuse me?"

"Never mind. So what makes you think that someone from North Muskegon killed him?"

"Oh we know. We just don't know who. I will be talking to Dr Prentice about her report. Look sheriff we are on the same side here. We both want what's best for your town. Now you can spend all of your time trying to figure me out or you could help me figure who killed Gaston. And catch Mufintano."

"Look, I want what's best for my town, they look up to me. I will be checking you out. But if you help me I will help you. What do you want to do next?"

"Ok. I have another agent in place watching people to see where things lead. But I need you to do just exactly what you have been doing."

"Fine but the next thing we have to figure out is who tried to off us last night."

"Yeah, something tells me that Mufintano is behind that one too."

"Look, I'm sure you're a good agent, I just...don't know...damn. Alright fine. But don't think that I won't be watching you. You are in my town, and his murder happened in my jurisdiction."

"Whatever you say 'sir'. But just so you know, if something happens and you can't control your people, it's your ass and the whole weight of the bureau will be coming down on you."

"I'm glad we understand each other. Now, we need to come up with a plan."

In what seemed like hours, Sheriff Garcia and AJ sat across from each staring and thinking about their next move. They both knew that Mufintano wasn't going to let up on his reign of terror. They also knew that if they didn't do something, someone they both cared about could end up like Yeager. Neither AJ nor Ray had to say anything, they both knew. Just when they thought it couldn't get any worse, the phone rang, "Sheriff, you have a phone call, line 1."

"Garcia."

"I know she's there sheriff. Just like I knew she was with you the other night. This is not your town anymore. There is nothing that happens here that I don't know about. So let me tell you something, you might as well pack up your so called reinforcements because they can't help you anymore. And don't worry about AJ, it's not her time yet. Good luck sheriff." Mufintano hung up and Sheriff Garcia lost all color.

"Sheriff? Are you ok? You look as if you've just lost your best friend."

"That was Mufintano and he told me that I am no longer in control of my town he is."

"Shit."

"Yeah that's not the worst part. He knows you're here."

"How?" AJ said as she now lost all her color.

"I don't know AJ. All I know is that we need to do something fast before this gets any worse."

"Any ideas?"

"You bring me as many agents as you can spare. This isn't about who's better than who anymore. This is about the safety of *my* town and the people I care about. You do whatever you can. God help us."

"I will push the panic button. Hopefully it won't take them too long to get here."

With that, both Ray and AJ got up from their seats, shook hands and walked out towards the front door. Both of them were hesitant to get into their cars, simply because of the earlier explosions. Garcia now knew there was a leak, or how else would Mufintano know that AJ was here? Sheriff Garcia couldn't shake the feeling he had about AJ. He still wasn't sure if he should trust her but at this point Sheriff Garcia didn't really have much of a choice.

"AJ, are you sure that you only have one other agent in place?"

"Yes. Quantico only sent two of us down here, why?"

"No reason." Garcia said as he watched AJ get in to her SUV.

Before AJ drove off, Sheriff Garcia gave her one last warning and he meant it

"AJ?"

"Yeah?"

"Watch your ass!"

Chapter 30

"Sheriff. We found the murder weapon. Well one of them anyway." "Ok I will be right there."

Sheriff Garcia got up from his chair, paid the tab and left. *Who needs to eat anyway?*

He thought he would eat and watch to see if anything was amiss at Rosie's Cafè. There was the normal hustle and bustle of a little coffee shop; locals stopping in for their everyday brew and catching up on their local gossip.

The staff was always the same save for Taryn. *Was this her day off?* Something was not right about her and the sheriff knew it. He couldn't make up his mind on what it was about her but something was definitely off. It seemed like he knew her, but couldn't remember how.

"Ok Kirby. What the hell is so pressing that you have to interrupt my lunch?"

"You wanted to know when the report came in from CSU. Well they found the murder weapon that was used to beat the hell out your victim."

"And you couldn't tell me that over the phone? I haven't eaten in God knows how long, only one cup of coffee this morning and I have a fucking town that's hosting the deliverance reunion. So just cut the shit and tell me."

"Do you feel better?"

"Man, you're about to get your ass kicked."

"You can't touch me and you know it."

Sheriff Garcia shot Kirby a look that would have suggested that Kirby was about to be one of the next unlucky ones if he didn't just get to the point.

"Ok fine. CSU found a baseball bat hidden in the bushes next to the rail trail behind the crime scene. It had blood and hair on it. The test results on the blood and hair conclusively link the bat to Yeager/Gaston. That's your murder weapon. Unfortunately there were no prints on it. But if you can find someone who was pissed off enough to want to beat a man to death............yeah yeah I know. Anyway, you have your hands full sheriff. But with what I told you earlier today, he wouldn't have put up too much of a fight because of all of the drugs that were in his system. That would also explain all of the blood that was found at the scene. With that many drugs in the system, his blood would have been more thinned out, add the beating and you have an instant bad paint job."

"Your sense of humor sucks ass you know that?"

"Yeah I know but with nobody to talk to but the dead, can you blame me?"

"Anything else?"

"Actually yes. Per your request, we ran blood tests on the three samples you gathered from your suspects and put them up against Yeager's/Gaston's and they all match. He was their father. All three of them!" Sheriff Garcia sagged down in to the chair like a lead balloon. "Are you sure?"

"Yes I am. Again, unfortunately."

He was not prepared to hear that. He didn't want to hear but there was nothing he could to prevent it, considering he wouldn't have ordered the tests to be run if he didn't suspect it.

Now, he had the added task of getting them together and ruling them out. Aside from Daphne, who already approached him about herself, his two other suspects were not going to go easily. He wasn't sure how he was going to deal with them. He knew that he was getting too close and the other one was getting too close to his daughter.

"Kirby. If I get you some more samples for further testing will you run them again but this time instead of the three young suspects will you run those against mitochondrial DNA?"

"Sheriff. What are you not telling me?"

"Nothing good. Look I don't want to tell anybody anything until I am 100% sure."

Kirby took one long look at the sheriff and he knew what Garcia was thinking.

"You think that the cases back in Jersey are related not only within that city but related to our case now. You think Yeager attacked those three women 19 years ago and he produced these three children. Holy shit."

"I never said that."

"You didn't have to."

The two men just looked at each other, stunned. Both of them knew what the other was thinking but were too afraid to speak about.

"Damn."

"Yeah."

"Kirby. Keep this to yourself until we know for sure, because if we are right, this is a whole new ballgame."

"No wonder so many people wanted that man dead."

"Yeah and the list keeps growing."

"Sheriff. Who do we trust at this point?"

"Nobody." With that last comment, Sheriff Garcia walked out of the lab stunned beyond belief.

"Director Colbert. I know we were supposed to meet but I have a situation here and there is no way that I can get away long enough to talk. Yes sir I know. I know that your agents were killed in my county. Do you really think I knew? What the hell are you talking about? You will not take this case away from me. I am close to cracking the whole thing wide open. Do not threaten me. Go to hell!"

Sheriff Garcia threw his cell phone across the seat and began mumbling. *Who the hell does he think he is? I don't give a damn if he is the director of a federal agency. Bastard. This is my case and it will remain my case. Sonovabitch.*

Sheriff Garcia kept wondering about Taryn and her absence. He wasn't sure but he knew that there was something about her. He knew that Director Colbert was really pissing him off and he also knew that he had enough to deal with without having to worry about the FBI director wanting to play in the sheriff's sandbox.

Garcia began thinking about Gaston and all of the information he heard from Dr. Prentice about Gaston's autopsy. *That had to be the only way. That's the only thing that makes sense. But what about Cecilia's murder, Jessica's attack and Jamie's attack?*

The more he thought about it, the more events seem to fall into place. All three women, at one time or another, had to all reside in the same city or within the same vicinity. Cecilia though, would have to be the last one to be attacked because everybody knew that after Cecilia's death, James left town, disappeared.

There were too many circumstances revolving around James Gaston that made Sheriff Garcia know in his gut who really killed James. But his gut was also bothered by the fact that nobody had really looked in to Brandie's parents. Why? Too many things weren't adding up and what about Jessica? He loved her totally but was it too coincidental that she was gone when he was killed?

Sheriff Garcia was wondering if he really was beginning to lose his mind. He wondered if he shouldn't turn the whole thing over to the feds and let them sort out the whole mess. But that thought was just temporary and decided nobody was going to take over *his* case. The answers to all of the questions kept rattling around inside his brain.

However, the one question that didn't go away was the reason behind the feds' car bombing. No matter how hard he tried, Sheriff Garcia couldn't make any sense of it. The thing that he didn't realize was that the answer would be closer than he expected.

Chapter 31

Kevin knew that he was getting close to being found out, yet he knew that if he didn't go through with his mission he wouldn't stand a chance to making it out alive.

Kevin was the type of person who usually didn't care what people thought of him. He never cared about the consequences before now; never cared who he would be hurting. But for some reason he feels like he has gotten an attack of good conscience. Why now? Not ever Kevin knew why.

A long time ago Kevin had a master plan. Follow his brother. And when he found out that James had fallen in with the wrong crowd, he had to do something about it. Especially when Kevin found out that the wrong person was Anthony Mufintano. He always felt as if he was his brother's keeper; ever since their childhood took its downward spiral after their parents' tragedy.

Kevin had the ultimate plan to finish high school and graduate college. But life had different plans for him. He ended up going into the Marines. It wasn't long before his leader noticed him and he was on a fire team. There were two others with him on the fire team and they were also excellent at what they did.

Over time they all went their separate ways but not before they had become involved in mercenary missions. None of them were proud of those choices but they did keep each other alive. After the three went their own way, Kevin had been recruited by the CIA. The CIA wanted Kevin because the special skills he developed in weapons and tactics while he was with the Marines.

Kevin had already done enough digging and found out that Mufintano was the one that killed their father so many years because dad wouldn't listen. The only reason he decided to accept the CIAs 'invitation' was because by then he knew that his brother was in deep with Mufintano. Luckily for Kevin, Mufintano didn't know who Kevin was and by then James was long gone. Kevin knew, or rather had his suspicions about what James had done to Cecilia and Theresa and he had a double mission. Stop Anthony Mufintano and James.

By then Kevin left the CIA and went off on his own volition to stop both men. He decided to go after his brother on his own time while still secretly working on bringing down Mufintano. There were times Kevin questioned his own mortality, wondering if he would ever make out alive. Now something to look forward to, he hoped and prayed he would.

"Sheriff. My name is Chris and I would like to meet with you as soon as possible." "I don't know you and frankly I have a lot to deal with right now so if you don't............" "Damn it sheriff I heard that you were a reasonable man. You will want to meet, trust me."

"A little arrogant aren't you?"

"I also heard that you were a bastard. You know what? Never mind. I also know that you are still looking for a second killer. When you feel like you can make the time to close this case let me know."

Chris was about to hand up his cell when the sheriff's voice stopped him.

"Wait! How the hell would you know that there were three killers?"

"Because sheriff, I was the other one. He was my brother."

There was a long pause, for what seemed like forever. Neither man knew what they should be saying next. Kevin wasn't sure if he should have said what he did and the sheriff wasn't sure if heard him right.

"Bullshit."

"Ok. If you don't believe me, that's your prerogative, just keep in mind when this is all over and you haven't caught Mufintano, you never will unless you accept my help. Good bye sheriff."

"Damn it. Wait. When and where?"

"In plain sight sheriff, see you in a few." and Kevin hung up.

Sheriff Garcia didn't know what to make of the caller but there was something about it that made him think that he knew him. It was the comment he made about plain sight. Whoever the caller was, was already getting on his nerves.

Sheriff Garcia was trying to get work done on his computer but kept thinking about the conversation he just had. He couldn't get his head wrapped around the name. *Chris?* Just didn't sit right.

"Sheriff, line one."

"Thanks." Before he could even pick up the phone, a man walked through the door.

"I told you. Plain sight brother." he said.

"Holy shit!"

"That's exactly right. Eu perdi-o demais meu amigo ?"

"We're not in Portugal anymore. English my man."

"So tell me Ray, how the hell did you get yourself mixed up with all of this? And why the hell did they appoint you sheriff anyway?"

"Kevin. Please don't tell me that you were the one that called me a while ago?"

"I cannot tell a lie sheriff."

Sheriff sagged back down in to his chair, not knowing how much worse this day could get for him. Two of his comrades were in town for God knows what and what he thought was a loyal employee had confessed to murder. Ray didn't know what to think of anything anymore.

"Always the smart ass." Ray said with a smile.

"Sim domine!" Kevin winked.

"Alright. What the hell is this shit about you saying that you killed my victim? I know you. You don't have any siblings."

"Ray. You only know what I wanted you to know. James Gaston *was* my brother. And many years ago, Mufintano killed our father."

"Bullshit. I don't..."

"That's your favorite word isn't it?"

"But how?" Ray looked like he had just seen a ghost.

"Short version? Mufintano killed our dad years ago and it was just by sheer coincidence that James got involved with him. I didn't figure it all out until the three of us, you, Ely and me, had gone our separate ways and I was working for spooks-r-us. I used that to my advantage to infiltrate the Mufintano family and I had been there for what seems like forever. I followed him here where I also found James. Once I got here, I caught him doing some bad things to people. I mean I had always suspected him of being not right but I couldn't face it until I seen it for myself. Look Ray, when I got to James he was already beaten, badly. I moved his body to his bed. Oh hell there was already blood all over. It was almost like the, beating started in bed and James tried to get up and run, but didn't make it. At that point their dog started to attack me and I had no choice but to defend myself......I am also the one who put the bowie knife in his chest."

Sheriff Garcia sat there staring at Kevin in total shock. He didn't know what to think in light of the information that he had just heard. At one time he trusted Kevin with his life and he Kevin was not the type of person to take anything lightly. He always trusted his gut and thought shit out, but right now the sheriff wasn't sure about anything, even Kevin's gut.

"Kevin I have a question and in light of all the shit you just told me, you better give me a straight answer. Have you kept in contact with Ely?"

"Yes I have. Not on a regular basis like calling him every week but I still keep in contact. Why?"

"I need to know. Does Ely have any children that I don't know about?"

"Where are you going with this Ray?"

"Kevin just tell me before I have you thrown in jail for murder."

"You're not serious?"

"Yes Kevin I'm dead serious. I need to know because I have a federal agent whose life depends on it. Now answer my fucking question."

"Geez ok. You're getting testy in your old age you know that? Yes, Ely has an illegitimate son by a one night stand. Him and her 27 years ago got drunk and one thing led to another or so the story was that he told me. Ely lost track of him. The last time he had contact with his son was 6 years ago. His son was fresh out of the police academy."

"What is his son's name?"

"I can't remember. That conversation was a long time ago. I think he said his first name was Eric. Ray, why do you look like you just saw a ghost?"

Sheriff Garcia just sat there again watching Kevin. For the first time in his life he felt speechless. He had no clue what to say or what to do next.

"This ends here. Now. You stay in town Kevin. I don't want to have to go after you too. There is a Super 8 around the corner. Make yourself comfy. I will call you soon."

Both men got up, shook hands and Kevin walked out of the sheriff's office. Kevin knew that now he came forward he would be watched closely. He knew the sheriff would also make sure that nothing would happen to him. Sheriff Garcia knew that if there wasn't any level of truth to Kevin's statement, he wouldn't have come forward to begin with. He knew that from his past there were only two men in the world he could trust. And now, they were both looking to him to be the one that saved them.

Chapter 32

"Sheriff, I think I have found a connection between the two car bombs. They were both made by the same person. The Tahoe that the two feds were in was blown up the same way as the Tahoe that Agent Ritter had been driving. Someone went through great lengths to make sure that these men, well at least the first two, didn't make it out. As for Agent Ritter, he just got lucky."

"Butch, is there anything else? How exactly did our madman create this bomb? Am I looking at an expert? Or someone who just had dumb luck?"

"Sheriff I doubt anybody could get this lucky. This was a well-planned piece of art. Both vehicles were wired the same way. The only difference is that Agent Ritter got lucky. He must have been smart enough to realize that when his truck didn't start on the first crank, something was up and must have tried to jump out right before the explosion."

"That still doesn't tell me what the hell happened Butch."

"Sorry. Whoever did this, wanted to make sure that there could be no evidence. But they screwed up. I found remnants of C4 still attached to the frame."

"You mean to tell me that whoever did this went through the trouble of getting ahold of C4? You know how hard it is to get ahold of that shit? No normal person can get it outside military channels. Who the hell are we dealing with here? *Sonovabitch.* Are you sure?"

"Yes sheriff I am sure. I have already sent samples to the local FBI office. I don't know what Robert Yeager did in a former life, but my guess is that he pissed off someone in purgatory."

"You have no clue."

"Excuse me?"

"Never mind. Keep looking over those trucks to see if you can find anything else. I don't want this bastard to get away with anything. You understand?"

"Yes sir. I will let you know if I find anything else."

"Please do. And do not talk to anybody else. Do not tell anybody anything. I don't want any unwanted rumors floating around town about anything."

"No problem. And sheriff..."

"What?"

"Watch your ass."

"And you the same." Sheriff Garcia said as he walked out of the police garage.

They both knew that this was now no simple school yard fight. This was a full blown war that was far from over. But what neither one of them realized was that it was going to take more than a little evidence to stop the monster who created this realm of insanity.

Sheriff Garcia drove back towards his office where he knew the CSU team was. He wanted to make sure that weren't going to miss anything. "Are you and your team still outside my office? Yeah well you better not even think about leaving until you have gone over everything. I know you know how to do your jobs but you have to understand two feds are dead and a third is knocking on deaths door. You do not leave until you have gone over every single inch of that scene!" the sheriff hung up and kept driving. Even though he would be at the crime scene shortly he wanted to make sure that the CSU team knew he meant business.

"Yeah, Garcia. What?" he said with an exasperated tone.

"What the hell are you talking about? What did you forget to tell me? What watch? Just spit it out. Fine explain it when I get there." he hung up and threw his cell in the to the passenger seat.

Sonovabitch it better not rain. Garcia kept looking towards the sky as he was driving. Seeing the dark cumulonimbus clouds moving in, he knew that is was only a matter of time before it would down pour. The skies were almost all black even though it was late afternoon and the winds started to pick up; indicating that a huge storm was on its way. He knew that if he didn't make it back to the station before it rained to help the team with the crime scene, he would lose any and all evidence forever.

Pulling in to his normal parking spot, Sheriff Garcia noticed that there was shards of glass and metal not fifty feet from him. He carefully stepped out of his vehicle and walked gingerly towards where the lead CSU member was standing.

"So now that I am here, tell me what you tried to tell me ten minutes ago."

"Sheriff I don't' know what Butch has already come up with at the garage, but we found a partial watch face. And if I was a betting man I would say that this is traces of C4 stuck to it."

"Sonovabitch. Is that it?"

"No. We've also found purple wires littered across the parking lot. I've already had one of my men bag it all up and take it to Butch so he could make some sense of it before it goes to the lab. Sheriff I don't like this. What the hell is going on here? It wasn't just two weeks ago that our town was quiet and boring. Now it looks like something Oliver Stone would have thought up."

"I don't like it either. It seems an expert in explosives is involved and they're not afraid of getting caught. Just make sure that you don't miss anything."

"Sheriff, one more thing. The watch had some engraving on it. I couldn't read it but I sent the pieces to the lab. Hopefully they can get some trace off of it and tell us what the engraving says."

"You couldn't read any of it?"

"No sir and it's not like I carry a magnifying glass with me."

"Everybody's a comedian. Look, if you find anything else call me and nobody else. Understand?"

"Yes sir."

"I think we should all be concerned and careful! No telling where this madman's ride is going to take us next. Finish what you were doing and I will call you later."

"Ok. When I get done here I will personally go to the lab to make sure that nothing happens to all of the evidence."

"Thank you."

After the two men were done talking, Sheriff Garcia walked into the building making a bee-line for his office. He spoke his pleasantries to the deputy posted outside his door, and walked in. *Doesn't look like anybody has been in here.* The town had been on edge ever since Robert Yeager's death and even the sheriff wasn't taking any chances.

After checking his room for any type of death creating devices, even looking under his chair before sitting down to think about what to do next. He knew Mufintano was behind all the death and destruction, but how he was going to prove it would be difficult.

It's not like he could walk up to the man and ask him. He knew that Mufintano had pelotas de latón but he didn't think that Mufintano would out right tell him. He knew that the Godfather was slicker than that.

Just then a thought popped in to his mind. Mufintano has no clue that Deputy Sherman isn't dead, and Garcia was going to use it to his advantage. It was his only trump card and prayed to God that it would work.

Chapter 33

Butch had to confess. He couldn't take it anymore. He beat the living hell out Robert Yeager so badly that he heard his bones crack. He couldn't stomach the fact that a sick bastard like him, was so close to the people he had learn to love.

Sitting in Sheriff Garcia's office Butch just sat there staring at a picture of the state flag on the wall behind the sheriff's chair. He knew he did wrong, but he didn't care. The only thing he cared about was that his newly found sisters and others would finally be safe.

The door opened behind Butch and he turned around to find the sheriff walking through it. "I understand that you want to talk to me?" Sheriff Garcia said as he sat down.

"Yes sir."

"Well about what? I don't have time that I can waste. I have an investigation that is about to put me in an early grave and you sitting in front of me instead of being in the garage working on the car that charcoaled two federal agents. None of the less is getting any easier for me because I can't figure out what the hell is going on with anybody. So now, after my little tirade, what did you want Butch? Have you found out what caused that explosion in that car?"

Wow. He thought to himself. *Maybe I shouldn't be here right now.* "Sheriff, I haven't figured out what specifically set off that explosion but I am here to talk to you about Robert Yeager."

"Ok. Shoot."

Butch kept rubbing his sweaty palms on his thighs and could barely make eye contact with the sheriff. Finally he just blurted it out, "Sheriff. I killed Robert Yeager!"

"Butch quit fucking with me. I have known you for years. You couldn't or wouldn't hurt anybody. I mean you can be an asshole but no way."

"Thanks for the vote of confidence but I killed him. I beat him to death. I couldn't handle the fact that he was doing such nasty things and especially to my sister. He needed to be stopped."

Sheriff Garcia couldn't believe his ears. A man he would be willing to call his friend, was sitting in front of him confessing to murder. It was very hard to believe.

"Butch, what the hell are you talking about? You couldn't have killed him, you just couldn't have........." Sheriff Garcia's voice drifted off, not knowing what to say or if he could trust himself to speak.

"Look, I admit that I did it. Sheriff, you just have to promise me one thing. You make sure that my sisters are ok. Neither of them did anything. I killed him on my own."

"Butch. Do you know what you're saying? If you confess, you will be arrested and charged. And there will be nothing that me or anybody else can do to help you. So I have to ask you, did you kill Robert Yeager?"

"Yes." Butch said officially.

Sheriff Garcia calmly picked up the phone, called booking and told them that he had a suspect in the Yeager murder and that he was in his office. It didn't take no time at all before two uniformed officers came in to the sheriff's office and formally arrested Butch. "You have the right to remain silent. Anything you say can and will be used against you in a court of law. If you cannot afford an attorney..." the officer was saying as he cuffed Butch with his hands behind his back and led him out of the sheriff's office.

"Wait! Butch I have one more question. How did you know that Cassie and Daphne were your sisters?"

"You have your sources sheriff, and I have mine." With that being said, Butch was led away and Sheriff Garcia was left alone, wondering what the hell just happened.

I just can't believe it. He couldn't have. He....why.....damn it! Ray got up from his chair and walked towards the door. Wondering who was going to be next in this twisted sick game.

Sheriff Garcia walked through the station where they were booking Butch. He stood there and watched as they printed him and took his picture. Ray still couldn't believe that a trusted employee and friend killed anybody. "Sheriff you know you shouldn't be here right now." Someone said.

"I know but he had good intentions." He whispered.

"Excuse me sir?"

"Never mind. Just make sure that you treat him with some respect and that you also go by the book."

While Sheriff Garcia waited for them to finish with Butch, he sat in the hall and began thinking about the whole scenario and what he could have done to prevent anything. The rational part of him knew there was nothing he could have done. But he also felt like none of this would've happened if he hadn't taken the position of sheriff fifteen years ago.

"Sheriff? They're done with Butch if you wanted to go in and talk to him. But I hope I don't have to remind you that they're ears everywhere."

"Who are you talking to? I am the one that had the damn things installed. Or have you forgotten?"

"No sir."

"Good, now get out of my damned way."

Garcia walked into the interrogation room, sat down and stared at Butch.

"You know why I am here. So why don't you tell me what happened."

"Sheriff I already told you, I beat Yeager."

"Yeah see that doesn't really cut it. I know you said that you beat him but you didn't tell me anything else. So let's try this again. What the hell happened?" Sheriff Garcia was all business. Straight faced no fluctuation in the tone of his voice. He was in charge and he made sure that Butch knew it.

"I saw Yeager walking the highway one day and I followed him home. I just wanted to talk to him, I swear. But anyway, he was already drunk or something because he was slurring his words. But one thing led to another and then the next thing I know he was swinging at me. What was I supposed to do? I had to protect to myself."

"So you expect me to believe that you were just defending yourself? You beat him? To death? That's one hell of a stretch Butch. That kind of beating suggests anger, and a lot of it. Look if you tell me that you didn't mean to do it, I might believe you. If you told me that you didn't have his reputation in your head when you were beating the shit out of him I might believe you. But tell me something real here."

"Sheriff, I swear. I did not intend to go there for the sole purpose of killing him. Sure I was pissed off for what he has been doing to my sisters; I just wanted to scare him. One question though; why the hell is one of the most feared mob bosses of all time in our town sheriff? What does he want?"

Sheriff Garcia just looked straight ahead at Butch blankly. He wasn't sure if he should tell him what was going on. He didn't know if Butch was just playing stupid or if he truly did just beat the guy out of anger. "Butch, I'm not really sure myself. But now I have a question for you. How did you know that she was your sister? I mean you had to have known that Cassie was your sister way before you killed Yeager. And you had to have known what he was doing to her. So how the hell did you find out?"

"All I can say sheriff, is I have better connections than you think." The two men just stared at each other trying to see who was going to blink first.

Chapter 34

Butch O'Niel was the prime suspect. Even though he had confessed to killing Robert Yeager, they still had to go through the legal steps of convening the Grand Jury and finding the jurors. And considering the gravity of the case and what he had done to so many people it would be almost impossible to find and impartial jury.

Sheriff Garcia knew he had his work cut out for him. The worst part is that he knew his suspect felt justified. He knew that Butch was doing what he thought was right. But it still didn't make it easier and in some respects didn't make any sense. His employee and friend is sitting in a cell awaiting trial for murder. And it didn't help knowing there still was a madman on loose with his psychotic cronies waiting to stop anybody that was stupid enough to get in their way.

Butch admitted to killing Robert Yeager but it didn't make any sense about the car bombs. He knew that Butch was a crackpot mechanic, so why would he risk putting any more heat on himself by blowing up the agents? Why would he kill the agents anyway? The sheriff understood why he would want Yeager dead, but what is the deal by killing the agents? None of that made sense. He had the feeling that Mufintano was behind the agents' killings, somehow.

Sheriff Garcia knew Mufintano was not the type of person to just stand there and let him close in on him. Right now everybody was in a big power struggle; the issue was who was going to be the first one to screw up and get caught?

He didn't know which way to turn first. He knew he had to take care of the mess with Butch but he also had Mufintano and the deaths of the agents and the car bombs. Not to mention the fact that his daughter, was about to face this whole mess alone since Jessica had her own problems to deal with which included her so called husband laying on a cold slab in the morgue because he pissed off more than one person. This whole town was turning in to one great big circus.

"Sheriff, line one."

"Thanks."

"Garcia."

"I know Butch confessed to Yeager's murder."

"Good for you. Are you ever going to tell me who you are? Or are we going to keep playing this song and dance?"

"Maybe. Mufintano needs to be stopped or you all are going to have worse problems. Do you know where your beloved daughter Cassie is?"

"Who the *fuck* is this?" Sheriff Garcia was getting really pissed off now just at the mere thought of some bad ass saying *his* daughter's name.

"Don't worry about it. Soon enough you will find out and then nobody is going to like it."

"Why don't you come in and we can talk about this? I promise to put away all of my weapons."

"Do you really think I am that stupid? And this line is not a landline and can't be traced."

"Why don't you tell me your name? You can do that can't you?"

"Nope. Not a chance. But I will tell you this, the alcohol tax in this city sucks." and then the caller hung up.

Everybody's a wise ass. Sonovabitch. What the hell's next? I'm tired of this shit. Picking the phone back up, Sheriff Garcia decided he had had enough. "Ely? I need your help. How quick could you get here? You know I wouldn't have called you unless this was important. You are the only one that could get me through this bullshit. Meet in my favorite place tomorrow about four. Yeah I know. I owe you one, again. See ya."

After making the one phone call Sheriff Garcia really didn't want to make, he sat back down and thought what the hell he was thinking by calling one of his old mercenary buddies. What was that going to prove? He was the sheriff for Christ's sake. He couldn't go about killing who he wanted to anymore just because they pissed him off. That would make him no better than Mufintano. *Damn it.* He knew that by now

Ely wouldn't be anywhere near his phone so it wouldn't do any good to try and call him back. All he could do was hope and pray that Ely would say no because he knew how he worked. Ruthless, once he set his mind on something.

Trying to turn his thinking back on to the unknown caller, the sheriff was looking over some of the reports from the explosion that killed the two agents. He felt like there was something there that he was missing but couldn't put his finger on it. He knew that the whole thing was connected somehow. If it wasn't for the fact that Butch confessed to Yeager's murder he would have enlisted his help. For now he would just have to use Butch's earlier reports and hope and pray that there was something in there he could use. Not to mention the fact Deputy Sherman wasn't Deputy Sherman but a special agent for the FBI none of whom he didn't trust. Sheriff Garcia had one hell of a mess going on.

All he could do was think if he could trust his gut or if he should go by the book. Neither of which was good right now. But he had to do something or else Mufintano was going to win and he didn't want that to happen.

Garcia began searching on his computer to see if he could find anything online about Mufintano. One thing that stood out was the fact that in every hyperlink when he typed in Mufintano's name, his daughter's murder came up along with something about a bank robbery. That just made the sheriff more confused. So he wrote down the name of the bank where the robbery occurred and started looking up that story. It didn't take long before he found a plethora of links for that. 'Cecilia Mufintano killed during botched bank robbery' was the most common headline.

Holy shit. No wonder Mufintano is so pissed off. But what did that have to do with Gaston? As his exhaustive to search turned up nothing further. He knew what had happened but not the details. Mufintano's daughter and wife were dead and somehow it all lead back to Gaston.

Reviewing the facts showed the robbery happened before Theresa's death. He printed out both stories and then laid them out on his desk. He stared at them so hard his eyes started to cross. He rubbed the bridge of his nose, then his eyes, took a drink of his coffee and resumed reading.

It didn't take long before he was seeing what he wished he could have seen so long ago when this whole thing first started. He finally made the connection between both stories. James Gaston had worked for Mufintano. Gaston must have fallen in love Cecilia and she knew it and when she spurned his advances, he had her killed. *She was telling the truth.*

It didn't take long before he figured out the rest. After Gaston killed Cecilia, he skipped town. Thought he was safe. But knowing his fetish for the ladies he set his sights on Theresa, only he didn't know that she was his Mufintano's daughter. She told him off or something and he went ballistic. It said in the papers that it looked like a love hate type struggle. It must have been then the FBI got involved. They put him in the program and that's how he ended up here. Mufintano must have tracked him down and that's why he's here. That would sure as hell explain why Mufintano was to do the hit himself. *Oh shit.* Garcia said to himself. *We're in trouble.*

Now Sheriff Garcia was really getting nervous knowing how everything was tied together. The one thing that he didn't quite know yet was if Ritter was on the take. If he was on Mufintano's payroll, that would explain a lot. Considering he didn't believe in coincidences. He really didn't want to have to arrest or worse off, shoot Agent Ritter. He had become extremely tired. The sheriff knew that sometime soon this was all going to come to a head and when it did, if people were smart, they would be somewhere else.

Chapter 35

Garcia knew that there was four manners of death but what he didn't know was that there were only two people responsible for his Robert/James' death. Sitting at his desk the sheriff kept thinking about the events that had happened surrounding Robert/James' murder. He didn't know that one of those people was closer to him than he would think. The only other thing that he had to worry about besides Mufintano was figuring out who actually bombed the feds.

Too many variables didn't add up. The unknown fingerprints, tox screen, missing file, the watch and starter, and what the hell is Ely up to? He was acting too 'helpful'. Ely never jumps into something he hasn't completely researched. The sheriff felt more suspicious of the people he should be protecting.

"Hello."

"Sheriff is Kirby back in the lab. I have the results you have been waiting for on the tox screen and all the fingerprints."

"Alright. I will be there in a minute." Sheriff Garcia was dreading the long walk from his office to the lab. It wasn't because he had to walk but it was because he wasn't sure if he had to hear the answers he was waiting for.

"Sheriff. I don't know what to think about all of this. The preliminary findings showed Agent Ritter's prints being on the knife that was sticking out of Roberts/James' chest when you found his body. But after further examination, we were wrong. Those prints weren't Ritter's. I mean both set of prints came from the same person but they didn't come from the person you expected."

"What the hell are you saying? Who did they come from?"

"You're not going to like this but....."

"Damn it just tell me!"

"After running the prints through AFIS for you, we have found out that they didn't come from Agent Ritter. They came from a man named Chris Sutton a.k.a. Kevin Gaston."

When Sheriff Garcia heard that name he felt like he was going to pass out, luckily he was already sitting. *This can't be happening.* "Are you sure?"

Kirby didn't know that the sheriff had already been in contact with Kevin Gaston, the decedent's brother.

"Yes sheriff, I am sure. Whoever killed your victim here is also the one that set the bombs that killed two federal agents. And that's not end of it. I also got the results back from the tox screen. There were high levels of Methadone and Xanax in his system. My bet is that somebody else wanted that man dead."

"Are you trying to tell me that I have two different murder suspects?"

"It looks like sheriff. Whatever that man did, he really pissed off a lot of people."

"If you only knew the half of it."

"I'm sorry?"

"Never mind. You keep this between us for right now. I can't afford for this information to get in to the wrong hands."

"Yes sir. If you say so."

"I need to go find Tracie....."

"Sir? There is one more thing that I almost forgot to tell you. The engraving on the back of the watch, we traced it back to the Marines."

"Excuse me?"

"The engraving on the back of the watch says 'Semper Fi Trio'"

Again the sheriff looked as if he was losing all color. *How could this day get any worse? Leave it to Robert/James to fuck up a good dream.* Luckily Kirby didn't hear the good sheriff. Because if he heard Sheriff Garcia would need to explain himself, and there was no way he could do that knowing only three people out there that had that same watch; Sheriff

Garcia was one, Ely was another and apparently the decedent's brother was another. They were the trio. The three of them served in the same Marine unit in the Special Forces. When they were there, they were inseparable. They covered each other's asses. It wasn't until this whole mess started that he started to remember anything. Once a Marine, always a Marine. *Semper Fi.*

He wondered what he was thinking by asking Ely to come and help him. What the hell was he thinking? Now he knew why Ely had been so anxious to help him.

"Ok thanks Kirby. If you find out anything else let me know. Remember that you have to keep this to yourself, especially if more feds show up. Right now I have no clue who I can trust. Understand?"

"Yes sir. And sheriff?"

"Yeah."

"Please end this. I don't know how much more I can take before I start smoking again."

"Funny."

"I try."

Sheriff Garcia left the lab feeling like he had been run over by a Mack truck. He knew that the Yeager/Gaston cases was not going to be an easy one but never imagined it would come back full circle and bite him in the proverbial ass.

Arriving at the department, the media circus was still camped out at any and all available spots. They wanted to make sure they were the first ones to bring the breaking story to their tables. He hated the media. He hated the thought of talking to them but he knew sooner or later he would have to say something.

Getting out of his cruiser he only spoke on sentence to them all, "No comment."

There were flashes going off and microphones being shoved in his face which only made him more upset. Don't they understand that I can't give out any information until we know everything?

"Sheriff. Daphne Alexander called for you. She said that she needs to talk to you as soon as you have free minute."

"You're kidding right? Do you think that I will ever get a free minute?"

"Don't shoot the messenger." the desk sergeant said and walked away

Damn it. This was getting out of hand. *Does anybody have anything better to do than to fucking gossip around here?*

"Sergeant? Did Ms. Alexander say where she can be reached at?"

"Yes sir. She said that you can reach her at work."

"Thank you."

Sheriff Garcia walked in to his office and slammed the door shut.

He knew he had his work cut out for him but he never thought he would ever get implicated. Even though he knew he wasn't touched yet, when the feds got a hold of this, he was done for. And he didn't want them to take over so if he didn't stop this now....well he didn't like the thought of the outcome.

"May I speak with Daphne please?"

"She's busy right now. Can I take a message?"

"Yeah just tell her that it was Sheriff Garcia returning her call. Tell her that I will be in my office for the next couple of hours if she still wants to talk."

"Ok thanks sheriff. I will tell her." and then the line went dead.

He was only mildly concerned that Daphne wanted to talk to him, but he had more important issues to deal with.

"Hello?"

"Sheriff?"

"Yes this Sheriff Garcia. Can I help you?"

"This is Kirby again. I just got the results back from that test you wanted on the Gatorade bottle."

"Do I need to be in person again or can you just tell me over the phone?"

"The Gatorade was spiked with the same drugs as the ones that we found in Yeagers system. Lethal levels nonetheless."

"Shit."

"That's what I thought. So I ran them again just for argument sake. And again, it came up the same. Lethal levels of Methadone and Xanax. Somebody wanted to make sure that he was good and dead."

The whole picture was becoming clearer for Sheriff Garcia. He was beginning to figure out the whole scenario and he knew it wasn't a pretty one. *The Gatorade wasn't meant for Cassie. She was telling the truth. She was just a 'wrong place, wrong time' type of situation. She was thirsty. Somebody wanted to make sure that Yeager was going to stay dead. That just means that he could have been poisoned at any time. He could have been poisoned the day before he was found. Damn it. That also means that Kevin is not the original killer. Who fucking poisoned Yeager?*

"Sheriff? Do you always talk to yourself or just on special occasions?"

"Excuse me?" he said looking up. Not realizing that Daphne was standing right in front of him.

"You were talking to yourself. They told me that you called me at work but they let me go early because we were slow so when I left I came straight here."

"Oh thanks. I just have been a little preoccupied."

"Really? You think?"

"Great another wise ass!"

"Sorry sheriff. You are just not the only one that has been under a lot of pressure and stress here. My brother and sister are suspects. People in town are so suspicious that nobody talks to their own neighbors anymore. So you will have to excuse me if I am just not in the nice mood category today."

"No, I am sorry honey. You're right we are all under a great amount of stress lately and …….." sheriff looked at Daphne with the most quizzical look on his face.

"Wait a minute. What do you mean your brother and sister? You're any only child."

"Damn it. I don't know what I am thinking. You're right. I am an only child."

"No. Talk now. That was no normal Freudian slip there."

"Sheriff. Butch and Cassie are my brother and sister well half-brother half-sister."

"But how? I mean I know how but how did you find out?"

"My mom, before she died, wrote a letter to me to be read after her death. I just read it last week. In the letter she tells of being attacked years ago by a man that came out of nowhere after she was walking to her car after grocery shopping. Apparently I am the result of rape."

All Sheriff Garcia could do was sit there stunned. He never thought that he would hear so many terrible stories. But the more he thought the more he knew how this town was one big family reunion coupled with a little insanity mixed in.

"Sheriff, I am scared to push the issue but part of me needs to know who my father is and how I am related to Butch and Brandie. He knows because I have already talked to him about us being related but Brandie doesn't know anything. Hell I don't know. But something tells me that it all revolves around Robert Yeager."

"Daphne, what does your family have to say about it?"

"Look sheriff, I have been on my own for a long time. And as I said, my mom died when I was young. I just need your help. Cassie is my friend and she trusts you."

"Ok. I will look in to it, but no promises considering I have my plate full now."

"This I know."

Daphne walked out of Sheriff Garcia's office feeling a little better but still unnerved by the whole situation and the sheriff was becoming more confused by the second. He wasn't about to tell her that he felt the same way she did, Yeager was the center of it all. But he still had to make the connection between all of the women, the attacks and how the three of them were all related. Still though, his first top priority was his own daughter. *Nobody will touch you, I promise.*

Chapter 36

Dr. Prentice proved to Sheriff Garcia that there was more than one person who wanted Yeager dead. And she also proved that any one of those people who wanted him dead had their own way of killing him. The kicker was that any one of those methods could have killed Yeager on its own. Sometimes Sheriff Garcia hated his job and often wondered why he chose to run.

He knew why. He had no family, no life so it would, at the time, be easy to be an elected official into a high office. Nobody to worry about if something happened to him. But now everything has changed. Garcia found out he has a daughter and there is a crazy man in his town. What the hell happened here? Yeager was dead, mob boss is in his town wreaking havoc, best friend and daughter are suspects. And he's the sheriff having to straighten out the whole mess, priceless. *Sonovabitch!*

"Sheriff? The hospital is on line one for you."

"Thanks."

"This is Sheriff Garcia."

"Sheriff, your deputy is finally awake. I know that you wanted to talk to him."

"Thank you I will be right there. Is his security detail still outside his door?"

"Yes sir. They have been there all morning. But there was somebody trying to go in to see him but I didn't know who it was."

"*What?* I thought I told you......"

"Calm down sheriff. I said that they tried. Nobody made it in. The officer outside his door wouldn't let him in."

"Nobody talks to him, nobody! Until I get there. You understand?"

"Yes sir." and then the line went dead.

Thoughts raced through his mind as he tried to figure out who the hell was trying to go in to see Agent Ritter's room. But unknownst to the sheriff, the person that was trying get in was going to wind up being closer to the whole investigation then anybody expected.

The hospital was full today. The ER was inundated with all types of people, from gunshot wounds to people who were just drug seekers. Considering the time of night it was, the sheriff had to go through the ER in order to get through to Agent Ritter's room.

"I was called from this hospital.............."

"Hold on sheriff." The nurse walked away briefly only to get on the phone to call up to the ICU.

"Ok. The charge nurse on the third floor is the one that you talked to. She said that your deputy is awake and wants to talk to you. Go straight down that hall to the end, turn right and the elevators would be on your left."

"Thank you."

The elevator ride seemed like it took forever. Not to mention that shitty music they always play. Wonder if it's there to test your strength of will?

Walking down the hall towards the ICU nurses' station, Garcia got a strange feeling in the pit of his stomach. He couldn't tell what it was but there was something wrong. "I'm Sheriff Garcia. I was told that Deputy Sherman is awake?"

"Yes sir. Just one moment." the nurse walked away briefly only to return with another nurse that seemed about ten years older than her.

"Sheriff, is there a problem?"

"No as I said to your nurse there, I was told that Deputy Sherman was awake and wanting to talk to me. Now if you could kindly tell me what room he is in and I will leave you to your business." Sheriff Garcia said as he began to get slightly irritated.

"Of course sheriff. He's in room 315. Private room. Just keep going down the hall and it's at the end on the right."

Of all of the times for someone to get scared of the badge. What the hell? Ray walked down the hall towards Sherman's room only to feel alarmed. *Where the hell is the officer posted to this room?* He thought. *I knew something was off.* Unsnapping his holster and drawing his gun, Sheriff Garcia hit the wall tight.

Just about the time he was going to kick in the room door, the officer came around the corner.

"What directly the fuck do you think you were doing?" the sheriff barked.

"I was using the rest room. Is that ok?"

"Do you think that you should be having that kind of attitude with me right now considering I could take your fucking badge? Or better yet, shoot you? What were my orders? Do you remember or were you just hoping that I would forget?"

"No sir. I just thought......"

"No that's the problem. You didn't think. I told you not to leave under any circumstances! He was your top priority. If you ever, fucking do that again while you were told to do something else, I will make a fucking example of you. Do you understand?"

"Yes sir."

"Now stand there like you were told until I tell you to leave." and with that, the berating was over and the sheriff walked in to see Agent Ritter.

Sheriff Garcia took a deep breath as he walked in and saw Doug hooked up to all of the machines and tubes. He never thought that he would care but he guessed wrong. In the short amount of time that Deputy Sherman has been with the department, he has touched many people, including the sheriff. But the sheriff was not about to admit it.

"Hey boss how ya doin?" Doug asked.

"I would ask you the same thing but I can kind of see. Are you in any pain? Do you need your nurse?"

"Look, sheriff. You don't have to tip toe around me. I've already been told I'll survive. It might take a while but the wounds will heal. So tell me what the hell is going on and who the hell tried to kill me."

"Well ok more to the point. Damn Sherman, do you think that maybe you should relax a little?"

"Sheriff, I want to know. I want to know who the hell is ravaging our town. There are too many people here that have been or are going to get hurt."

"You're a rookie. You don't have enough time in with us to........"

"To what? Care? Bullshit! Don't tell me that. I don't care if I am a rookie. I care what happens to your people and those around you."

"Why? Huh? Tell me that. What's in it for you?"

"What are you talking about?"

"You are acting a little too 'pushy' for a newbie. The only thing that makes sense is that you have more invested. So I'm asking you again. Who the hell are you?"

"I'm your deputy, sheriff."

"Good bye Doug." The sheriff got up and started to walk away only to be stopped by a comment that he wasn't prepared to hear.

"Damn it. I'm a federal agent! I told you once before. What more do you want?" Eric didn't know that Sheriff Garcia already knew all about it.

He turned around only to stare at Doug or whoever he was. "Trust me sheriff. I'm an agent. We can make anybody change. Think about it. Why do you think it seemed too 'neat' when you got my transfer papers? Why do you think you didn't have to do anything? We made it neat for you, so there would be no questions from nobody.

Sheriff, I'm an agent and probably the next one to die."

"Sheriff....."

"Look, they already think your dead. I covered your ass. Don't know why but I did.

Nobody knows you're still alive except me and some of the medical staff here. Even the press thinks you're dead. So tell me now, who the hell are you?"

"Sheriff, I told you. I am a federal agent. My name is Special Agent Eric Ritter and I was put here to *help* you. Not hinder you."

"Well, *Eric*. As I've said everybody thinks you're dead. So what are we going to do next?"

"I guess we plan a funeral." Agent Ritter said with a sly smile.

He hated having to figure shit out on his own.

"One thing, if you ever lie to me again, I will shoot you myself. My daughter is top priority here. And if Mufintano or anybody touches her I will kill them myself. Now, when you're feeling better we need to sit and talk and put our heads together to try and figure out what the fuck is going on. We need to figure out exactly what Mufintano's angle is with this whole thing." Even though Garcia already knew the truth.

"Well sheriff I can tell you one thing. It has to do with something that happened a long time ago between Mufintano's wife and James Gaston, then some years ago Mufintano's daughter and Gaston. I hadn't gotten that far before I was pulled and sent to you. I swear." *Maybe he was telling the truth.*

"We need to get to a computer. Hey what kind of pull do you have in the department? Do you think you could get someone looking for you? Is there anybody you trust in the bureau that could do your work for you?"

"Yeah there is one person that I would trust with my life. But I need a secure line to call them."

"Here use my cell phone. Nobody within the FBI would know it, they wouldn't suspect anything."

"Perfect. Just tell me one thing sheriff. Why would you want to try and be nice to me now?"

"Because we are on the same side, remember. Something is telling me that you want him as bad as I do. And if you do anything to jeopardize this and ruin it for my daughter, I will kill you myself. Good enough for you?"

"Fair enough." Eric said with a smile, "Now, give me minute to make my call."

While Agent Ritter was talking to somebody on the phone, Sheriff Garcia stepped in to the hall and began pacing. His mind began whirling, thinking about the many reasons why Mufintano himself would be in town. It made him want to find the bastard and wring is fricking neck.

"Sheriff, you got a phone call." the nurse said as he snapped out of his revere.

"Ok thanks." Walking up to the nurse's desk, he had an odd look on his face as he answered the phone.

"This is Garcia."

"Sheriff, we have a problem."

"What are you talking about?"

"The lab found something that I think you should see."

"No, you tell me now. I am busy and don't have time for random bullshit."

"Sheriff they found an unidentified set of prints on that watch they found at the scene."

"You interrupted me for that?"

"No sir. One of the other set of prints they found was matched to Deputy Sherman."

"Are you sure?"

"Yes sir. They said they ran it three times."

"*Sonovabitch.*"

Hanging up, the sheriff didn't know which way he should turn. Something was telling him that the labs were wrong. Or maybe it was just that he hoped they could be wrong. Turning around, Sheriff Garcia stood there trying to gather himself instead of bursting and painfully pulling every tube and line that is attached to whatever his name was.

"Everything ok?"

"Yeah. My contact within said that they would get looking immediately to see what they can dig up about Mufintano."

"Anything else?"

"No. Sheriff are you ok? You look a little *off*. You sure you're ok?"

"Yeah I'm fine."

"Ok. Then I guess the next thing we have to do is put a tail on Mufintano and his crew and watch them really close."

"Sounds like a plan to me. Just one thing though. Why do I get the feeling that there is something that you are not telling?"

"I'm not." with that being said both men just stood there staring at each other. Both of them were wondering who was going to blink first.

Chapter 37

He still couldn't believe it or didn't want to believe the *possibility* of Agent Ritter being on Mufintano's payroll. So far there was nothing that would make the sheriff think otherwise. Ritter was a good man and he was especially careful with Cassie when he questioned her, he was almost protective. Something just didn't add up. *Couldn't be*?

For his own peace of mind the sheriff began doing some digging on Special Agent Ritter. He thought that he had a better chance while Ritter was still in the hospital than trying to question the man face to face since he might not tell the truth anyway.

Thoughts ran through Ray's mind about his life, his newly found daughter, the life he could have had if not for the fact that Gaston took it all away from everybody. That man was a menace. And for a second, part of him was glad that he was dead. But as fast as he had the thought, he knew it wasn't how to deal with his kind.

Picking up the phone Ray looked outside only to see that the swarm of reporters was still there. *Damn it.* "Hey Jessica. Just checking to see how you two are doing? Are the two officers still outside? Good. I promise I will make this right for you when this is all over. I am so sorry. I know, but still you deserve better. Ok will talk to you later. I will stop by there sometime today. Alright, bye." His heart ached for the woman who made him feel whole. He was in love with her all over again.

Trying to return his thoughts back to how he was going to stop Mufintano, there was a knock on the door. "Come in."

"Sheriff."

"Doctor Prentice. To what do I owe this pleasure?"

"We need to talk."

"I thought that we did all the talking there was. You told me that there was more than one person who killed Yeager. You told me what each person did or used to kill him. So what else is there?"

"You left before I could tell you that whoever shot Yeager, was also diabetic."

"Yeah? And how do you figure? I mean I know that you're the doctor but how?"

"They found ketoacidosis in a soil sample."

"English doc."

"Whoever shot Yeager, where they shot him from, took a piss. So when your CSU was checking the crime scene, not only did they find spent shells, they smelled something fruity at the base of the tree from which he was sitting. That prompted them to check the soil."

"Holy shit. Are you sure?"

"Yes sheriff I am sure. I already had them run the tests again just to be safe."

"Is that it? Amazingly not."

"You're kidding me right?"

"No. Whoever shot Yeager, was also related to him."

Sheriff Garcia was stunned beyond belief. Even though Kevin admitted everything to him the sheriff was hoping that he had been lying. He couldn't believe that his town was as crazy as it was and he couldn't believe that one of the killers was related to the victim. What the hell is this place coming to?

"Are you sure?"

"Yes. The only thing I can tell you is that the suspect is male."

"Brother?"

"Possibly. Maybe a cousin."

"I can't......I don't know what.......damn."

"Yeah."

"Ok doc thanks. I guess I have a lot more work cut out for me than I thought."

"You got that right. I will let you know if I find out anything more."

"I don't know if I would want to know." Garcia said with a deep chuckle.

"No shit. Later sheriff."

Doctor Prentice walked out Garcia's office and they were just as stunned as if they both got hit with the same baseball bat. Neither one of them knew what they should say. Sheriff Garcia just sat back down carefully and continued to stare at the wall in front of him.

Great! The sheriff thought. Now he has to deal with a pissed off relative along with a psychotic mob boss and the possibility of a friend killing off special agents. He couldn't stomach the thought of Butch being a murderer let alone possibly working for Mufintano. He needed his daughter. He needed to talk to her to make sure that she knew that he didn't intentionally leave her. He needed to talk to Jessica so she knew that he loved her, that he still does. There was so much that he needed to do and say but yet it just seemed like there wasn't enough time.

The great sheriff was at a loss. He knew that he was running out of time for everything. He didn't know who he could trust. He didn't know where to go for help. Even with the thought of Ely coming brought uncertainty. Trust Ely? Maybe. Did he trust Ely to get the job done?

Absolutely. That is what bothered him the most. Once Ely set his sights on something, it was really hard to get him to stop. It was like taking a sick animal away from a rabid dog.

Ray was almost falling asleep sitting up when he heard a knock on his door. "Who is it?"

"Just open the damn door and find out."

Shit! Has it been that long already? He thought.

Getting up, the sheriff knew he was in trouble the minute he put his hand on the door knob.

"Hello Ely. Come on in. Have a seat. I thought I told you to meet me somewhere else?"

"Qué está arriba fucker? Tiempo largo no ve."

"Nice! Something's never change I see?"

"Ok you interrupt me and my much needed siesta and you're already getting on me? What the hell?"

"Ely, I need your help."

"Yeah this I gathered."

"I see that you haven't changed with age."

"And I see that you have changed with age!"

"What did you expect?"

"Look, have you watched the news at all?"

"About this place? No, why should I?"

"Perfect. This makes it easier."

"What the hell are you talking about?"

"I have a situation here and I need your help. Your expertise if you will."

"Oh this can't be good."

"Ely, there are some not nice people in my town that are wreaking havoc. There has been one hometown murder, two federal agents blown up from a car bomb right in front of my office; another agent is dancing with death from the same thing. Not to mention there is a refuted mob boss in my fucking town possibly behind it all. Oh and my daughter is one of the main suspects."

"Wait. What? You have a daughter? Since when did you still know how to......?"

"Focus man. I just found out. Anyway, I need your help. You're good at finding a means to an end."

"Yeah but the mob? You can't be serious? Man you really know how to muddy your shoes don't you? This mob boss, who is he?"

"Anthony Mufintano."

"You're shitting me right?"

"No." Sheriff Garcia said with a serious look that would make the Pope turn away.

"You don't need my help brother, you need the fucking Marines."

"Tell me about it. Why don't you think that I called you? So are you going to help me or what?"

"Well I can help you the best I can. But something tells me this is not going to turn out good for nobody. So what's your plan?" Ely asked.

"That's thing. I really haven't thought of a good enough one yet."

"Jesus Ray. What the hell were you thinking?"

"I don't know. But I need to do something quick before more people wind up dead. You're good at Black Ops, sniper shit. I need you to start watching Mufintano and his crew. Get to know his routine. You're also a whiz with computers I need you to look into someone named Eric Ritter."

"Special Agent Eric Ritter? What the hell does he have to do with all this? Is he the other agent you just mentioned that is close to death?"

"Ok, see, I really didn't hear that tone from you. What the hell, are you trying to kill me already? I'm afraid to ask this question, but how do you know Ritter?"

The sheriff already knew the answer to that question but he was hoping Ely would tell the truth.

"Let's just say that he and I had a difference of opinion some time ago."

"Great. Perfect. Maybe it would be better if you did go back home."

"Now I know you're on drugs if you think that I am leaving now after you told me all this!"

"Ely this isn't a game. There are real lives at stake."

"No shit. I know all about Mufintano and the bad shit that he can do. And by the way, how well do you know Ritter?"

"He just transferred in from; well he was a plant in my department. But I am still not sure who's side he is one. I don't know if I can trust him to be a cop or one of Mufintano's hinch men."

"Well I can tell you one thing, as a cop, the dealings I've had with him, he's as tight as they go."

It was the first time since Ely got there that neither of them said a word. Nobody knew what should happen next.

"Ely, is there anything that would suggest Agent Ritter shouldn't be trusted?"

"If I were to venture a guess right now, I would have to say no. If he's here, there is a damn good reason."

Both Ely and Ray were finally at a standstill with respects to the sheriff's town. They both knew that something had to be done. Neither one of them was sure about what should happen. Ely wasn't supposed to be there at all and the sheriff could lose his job if they knew he was the one that requested Ely's presence. But there was no one else the sheriff could trust in a situation like this. Now that he was here, what were they going to do?

Chapter 38

Who knew it was going to turn out like this. Not even *he* knew the magnitude of his actions. First the two agents, then Deputy Sherman. He didn't know how this whole thing was going to play out. But one thing was for sure, more people were going to die before Mufintano was done with his game of revenge.

Looking out over Muskegon Lake he could feel that he was getting too close. He should have never decided to get in bed with a man like Mufintano. He was smarter than that, or at least he thought he was.

He didn't know what he was going to do next. He knew that Mufintano was watching everything he did very closely. He also knew that his career was over the minute he accepted Mufintano's help. The bad thing was he didn't know the loan officer was really a mob boss until it was too late.

Too many times he tried to make his life better and it didn't work out, he thought. Leaving home at an early age, he thought, was good idea because the abuse he received at the hands of his father would be enough to screw up anybody's head. If his mother wasn't going to do anything about it, than he could and that's why he left. He often wondered what happened to his father. He heard through different relatives over time that his mother died after his dad went on a drunken rage one night. He regretted not going to his mother's funeral, but he knew that if he did, his father would be lying in the coffin next to his mother. Lighting a cigarette, he was thinking about what he could do to get out of the mess he created.

"Yeah."

"Where are you right now?"

"I'm sitting at the lake. Why?"

"The boss wants you, now."

"Fine. I'll be there in a minute." *Shit*, he mumbled to himself. Getting up he knew that whatever it was it wasn't going to be pretty.

While getting into his car, one thought kept going through his mind. *How long before I'm next?* He prayed as he turned the key. Hoping that he would live to see another day. He kept trying to think about a way out. He never knew what his life was going to be like, he never thought about his future. But then again, foresight was never his forte`.

Great! He thought. *Just what I need, another damn rainy day. I hate it. I frickin hate the rain almost as bad as I hate winter.* Turning on the wipers his mind raced in tune with the tempo of the wipers. There was no way he could safely get out from underneath Mufintano's grip.

Driving was the only thing that helped relax him. Being in control of his life, even if it meant only for a little while, helped him to see clearly. The fear of the unknown was the one thing he hated the most. Just when he thought it was safe, his phone rang. Looking at the ID he noticed that it was Cicero. *Shit. What now?*

"Yeah."

"Boss said change of plans. He will meet with you tomorrow. He said he had something to take care of."

"Ok. Same time?"

"Yeah. In his office. Don't be late."

Thank God. Now what? He changed his course and headed home. He knew that at least he had one more day to think about what story he was going to tell Mufintano when they met. All he could do was hope Mufintano couldn't tell he was lying, because if he did, he wouldn't live to see his next family reunion.

Knowing that he dodged the proverbial bullet, he had a little more time to figure out what he could do to save his own ass. He knew that he should have stayed home that night. But no, he had to prove that he was just as good as his brother and went and borrowed the money for the down payment on his new rolling bachelor pad.

Arriving home, he locked the doors to his over-priced Hummer and walked inside. The room seemed empty. The whole apartment seemed empty for that matter. At forty nine, he never felt so alone. Never had he imagined that he would be hoping for an easy way out. Always hoping that he would catch the eye of someone special. At one point in his life he thought there was someone special but she turned out to just be a passing fancy. She wasn't the person that he could give is whole heart to.

Walking in to the kitchen, he opened the fridge realizing that he only had one more beer left. *Damn it,* he murmured to himself. He sat down at that the table thinking about the days' events and wondering how much time he had left. He knew that Mufintano would spend no time on burying him. Hell, he figured Mufintano would do the dirty work himself just to make sure that everybody else would get his point. *God help me.*

He was too juiced to just sit still. He couldn't handle sitting home knowing that he didn't have much time left, so he grabbed his jacket and left. Driving he wondered where he could go to help forget about all of the hell he had gotten himself into through the years. Depression was a bitch.

The city looked like a ghost town tonight. But of course it was in the middle of the week.

Pulling in to the parking spot in front of Chuggie's, all he thought about was getting himself nice and tanked. He had no plans to for niceties. He just wanted to be a bastard and get drunk.

Sitting down at the bar, he ordered his normal Jack and Coke and slammed it the minute it showed. The bartender brought another drink almost instantly. "You having a bad day buddy?"

"You could say that. Just keep them coming."

"You got it. But just know that I will not hesitate to cut you off the minute you get stupid. Got it?"

"No problem. You want my keys now or later? Just know that if you say later you will have to dig into my pocket yourself." He said with a slight smile.

"Don't worry. I have my ways. I'll just cuff you to the stool and clean up around you."

He didn't know what to make of that comment. He just smiled and shook his head while the bartender went about her business. *Wow,* he said to himself. It was nice that for just a second he smiled and forgot that anytime soon, he was going to die at the hands of a madman.

Old school music was playing in the background. Styxx was a band that would forever be immortal and Chuggie's was the only place around where someone his age could still listen to the oldies.

He watched the bartender and one thought popped in to his head. And that kind of thought should be illegal in most states especially considering he was way older than her. What would she want with someone his age anyway? She was nice to him only because she was paid to be.

"Hey. It's about time."

"What are you talking about?" He asked the bartender.

"You're smiling. When you first came in here you looked like you wanted to kill someone."

"Yeah well, don't get used to it."

"Why not? It looks good on you." She said with a sly smile on her face as she walked away.

"So why are you having a bad day anyway?"

"Is there a reason you want to know? Or is just in your nature to be nosey?"

"Wow. That hurt. Do you feel better? Or is it just in your nature to be an asshole?"

For what seemed like a lifetime, they both just stood there looking at each other wondering who was going to blink first. Then all of a sudden they both just started to shake their heads and smile.

"Look I'm sorry. I just.......hell I don't know. Rough day, rough week. Shit rough life. Thank you for playing along."

"Any time honey. So now that you don't look you want to kill me. What's your name?"

"Just call me Chris."

"Well Chris, your glass is empty. You want another one or are you heading out?"

"Tell me your name and maybe I'll tell you what I'm going to do next."

"Oh, ok. You want to play that game? I see how you are. And what are you going to do if I don't tell you my name?"

"Cry like a baby." Chris said looking over his glass at her.

"I'll tell you my name if you tell me how old you are." She said after winking.

"You do not play fair honey. You know that right?"

"I never do."

"And if I refuse, you promise to cuff me?"

"So now who's not playing fair?"

"I love this song. Dance with me." Chris said while smiling and listening to Etta James.

She looked there staring at him, sporting a wide grin. "You promise to behave yourself?"

He took her hand "Never."

"Well then how could a lady refuse?"

"You can't." Chris exclaimed as he slowly wrapped his body around hers ever so gently.

For the first in his life, Chris actually, if only for a moment, felt something within him. He felt like he could enjoy life. But what difference did it make now; he knew he was going to die. And for the first time he felt like he had something to live for. But as quick as that thought came in to his head, he banished it. Why would someone like her want to have anything to do with him? He was too old, too used and he knew it. *Enjoy it why you can.* He thought.

She laid her head on his shoulder and closed her eyes. Unbeknownst to him, she felt like she didn't want to let go. He didn't know about her history. He didn't know how bad her life had been for her. The only thing that he knew was she was here, now. And her arms were around him just as tight as his were around her. Neither one of them knew that the other was right where they wanted to be, right where they needed to be. She felt for the first time in her life that he would be the one to save her. But what she didn't know was that this would probably be the first and last time she ever seen him.

"So are you ever going to tell me how old you Chris?" she mumbled in to his shoulder.

"Do you really want to know?"

"Yes." she said as she lifted her head to face him, to look him in the eye.

"Does is it really matter?"

"No. Not at all. If it bothers you that much, you don't have to tell me." She said as she smiled ever so gently and laid her head back on his shoulder. For a second he would have thought that he felt her tighten her grip around him.

Keeping the smile to himself, he caught himself stroking the back of her head and playing with her hair and then without thinking, he told her. "I'm forty nine."

"Excuse me?" she said lifting her head looking at him.

"I said I'm forty nine."

"Thank you."

"You're welcome. Will you ever tell me how old you are? Or do I have to guess?"

"Songs over and I have to get back to work." She said smiling the type of smile that could get him to do anything.

Chris went back to sitting on his stool and took another swig of his Jack and Coke. Elton John's 'It's still rock and roll to me' began hitting. "See, now who's not playing fair? Will you at least tell me what your name is?"

"You keep drinking like that and you won't remember it so why should I?" She said as she winked at him.

"I'll quit right now. I'll even give you my keys. But that just means that you will have to drive me home."

"Ok, ok. I give up. My name is Trista and I am thirty seven. Satisfied?"

"Thank you."

"You're welcome."

"Well thank you for the dance Trista. I better go. Got a long day ahead of me tomorrow." Getting up, Chris felt almost guilty for feeling something for someone who was so young, someone he had just met. What made it worse was that she acted like it didn't bother her. Either that or she was faking it really good.

"Leaving so soon Chris? What's the rush? What is so pressing that you can't stay a little longer?" Trista asked as she pushed the button to her favorite song in the jukebox.

"I just have things to do."

"You're bothered by my age aren't you?"

"No. Why would I?"

"Yes you are. Otherwise you would look at me."

"I just have to go. Thank you for your hospitality and the drink." Chris began to walk towards the door. He knew that he had to go before anything happened. He could feel it. He could tell that she wasn't bothered by his age. He also knew that if he didn't leave soon he couldn't be responsible for his own actions.

Before he knew it another slow song came on and she was right behind him. So close that he could feel her from breast to pelvis against his back. And then he felt her hands on his hips.

"Dance with me again." She whispered at the back of his neck. That melted him. He could feel himself begin to shake. *Damn it.*

Without thinking he turned around. He knew he shouldn't but he couldn't help himself. He felt alive for once in his life. And considering he probably wouldn't be alive too much longer, he figured he might as well make the best of a shitty situation.

Chapter 39

"Chris? Are you ok? You look a little flushed."

"Yeah I'm fine."

"Are you sure?" Trista asked as she nuzzled Chris's neck when she put her head on his shoulder. *Oh God help me.* Chris mumbled to himself. *You're beautiful.*

"I'm sorry?"

"Nothing."

"I love this song. I think Styxx is one of *the* best bands to ever grace our presence."

It wasn't until what seemed like forever before Chris realized that Trista was massaging his back in line with the tempo of Dream Weaver. He didn't know how much longer he was going to be able to contain himself. He was getting hotter. But what did he know, she was only the bartender and she was young and he was going to have leave town so he wouldn't see her again. Except he wasn't sure if he wanted to now.

In that moment, it was just them. The two of them on the dance floor enjoying each other's company. Not caring who what was going to happen next. Then before neither one of them realized the song was over and they were still holding each other.

"I think the song is over."

"I know."

"Trista, don't you have to go back to work?"

"Look around, do you see anybody here?"

"No but......" He started to talk but he was dumbfounded by the fact that she was ever so lightly brushing her lips on the side of his neck and he couldn't think and talk at the same time. He wasn't sure what bothered him the most. The fact that he never felt so alive, so aroused before or that it was a woman twelve years his junior and she liked him just the way he was.

I can't do this. Chris started to pull away from Trista but she stopped him.

"Don't." Trista just stood there looking at Chris with nothing but simple innocence in her eyes. He tried to tell himself that he was drunk. It couldn't be real, the feeling he was feeling. How could someone so beautiful, someone so full of vitality want anything to do with someone with the likes of him; a washed up, beat up shell of a man.

"Why?"

She didn't say anything. All she did touch was his ear and begin running her finger ever so lightly along the side of his face and that's all it took. Before she knew it he had her up in his arms up against the bar wall kissing her with so much force that neither one of them could breathe. *God forgive me.* He thought to himself.

Trista put both of her hands on both sides of his face and that calmed him instantly. He slowed his breathing and continued his passionate kiss on her. His tongue exploring every spot inside her and in turn, she was turning into putty in his arms. She was returning the favor by holding on tight.

He carried her to the bar where he sat her down on his stool and before he could think she wrapped her long legs around his waist and smiled up at him. "Hi."

"You're beautiful."

"So are you." she winked.

"I don't want to leave."

"Then don't." she said as she started kissing the side of his neck and nibbling on his ear.

"You're not making it easy for me you know that right?"

"I know. Stay here."

"I can't. I have something that I have to do tomorrow. As much as I am *really* enjoying myself right now, I can't miss it."

"Ok. Whatever it is, I am sure that it will all work out for the best."

"If only you knew. I would rather be here than there."

Trista put her hands on the sides of his neck and began rubbing his jaws. "Chris, nothing in life is easy. The choices we make only make us stronger in the long run. Whatever it is that you have to face tomorrow, something tells me that you will be ok."

Staring in to her crystal blue eyes, there was something there that told him she was right. He didn't get it. He couldn't figure it out. But he knew she was right. The other thing that he couldn't figure out was how, after just an hour he felt like he had meant his destiny. He didn't want to leave her. He wanted to make the world a safer place for her.

"How did you do it? I don't understand." he said as he stood there dumbfounded.

"Did what?"

"Never mind. Promise me something?"

"Anything." she said smiling.

"You will be here tomorrow?"

"Yes."

"Promise me?"

"Ok. I promise."

"Thank you." he said has he kissed her on the top of her head. "I really do need to go."

"I know." Trista winked and then kissed him full force as she tightened her grip with her legs around his waist. So tight that she could feel him press himself against her right where it counted and it inexplicably made her moan. And that in turn made him harder.

"You really don't care do you?"

"What are you talking about?" Trista asked with an odd smile.

"Never mind."

"You keep saying that." she said then she kissed him again.

"You keep kissing me like that and I won't ever leave."

"That's the plan."

"Funny. I have to leave Trista. But with any luck I will be back tomorrow. You'll wait for me? Or at least for one day?"

"You know when you smile like that, for a moment, my world is ok."

"Where were you all these years?"

Trista let that one go. But Chris could see the confused look on her face and wondered if he should ever venture in to the unknown with that one. He knew that now his life had purpose. It had meaning. And that in turn scared the hell out of him.

She walked him to the door and it was there that he let something slip. "I'm going to miss you."

But she never missed a beat. "I'll miss you too." And like she knew what he was facing tomorrow. She said one last thing that would stay with him until the end. "Stay safe."

With that being said, Chris grabbed her once last time and planted a long, hot kiss on Trista. His hands exploring every inch of her body, including her perfect, firm breasts. And that got him instantly hard, again. "Oh God help me. You have no clue what you are doing to me."

"I have a good idea." Trista said with a coy smile, "You need to go. I'm not going anywhere. You promise me something? You keep yourself safe. I don't know what you have to do tomorrow but something is telling me that it's not going to be good."

"You're right. It's not going to be good. But yes, I will try to be careful. Now I better leave before I really get in trouble."

"What makes you think that you would get in trouble here?" Trista asked while nibbling on his ear.

"See, that doesn't help. I was right, you are trouble." he said smiling.

"Ok, fine. But if you don't come back tomorrow night. I will come looking for you."

"Promise?"

Trista laughed, "Yes, I promise." With that being said, she planted one last hot kiss on him before he left. But unbeknownst to Chris, his life was going to be kicked in to high gear. He was finally feeling something for someone that he had never felt before and even though Trista was twelve years his junior he knew that she was the one to save him. But he had no clue that in the next few days, it would test his will as a man, skill to stay alive and Trista was the key to everything.

"You better come back Chris." she smiled.

"You can bet on it. Just watch your back and lock your doors." he said with a stern look.

Trista looked at him with a confused look on her face, but something inside her heart told her to listen, "I will. See you soon." and with that she blew him a kiss good bye as he walked away. She stood there knowing that there was a reason for everything and soon her beliefs would be tested, along with her fight for survival.

Driving home he kept thinking about Trista and what he had gotten himself into. He knew that he could just easily never go back. Chalk her up to nothing but a fun night girl and leave it at that. But the funny thing was his feelings were overloading his ass and he felt happy for once. He wasn't just letting his little brain run the show. He wanted her in his life. It was almost like he had known her his whole life and lost her somewhere along the way and just got her back. He knew that he wanted her, but something else was telling him there was a good chance that he wouldn't see her alive again.

Chapter 40

Chris knew he shouldn't have done what he did at Chuggie's. She was beautiful and outright hot but he also knew that the minute he became involved with her, he put her life in danger. What was he going to do knowing that Mufintano wanted his head on a platter and the sheriff expected order restored in his town? There was no way for him to live through this. He didn't know what he was going to do.

Driving back from town, he began thinking about his brother. He was dead and he had a hand in it. He could barely stomach the thought that he killed his brother but he had to be stopped. He knew that if he didn't, James would continue to hurt more people if Mufintano didn't get ahold of him first.

Chris began thinking about how they grew up.

"Come on James. You know that mom isn't going to do shit to you, just jump. You never get in trouble with mom. I always have to get my ass handed to me whenever either one of us does anything. Mom likes you best, and you know it."

"That's not true. I get in trouble just as much as you do."

"Yeah ok. Whatever, just jump or I'll push you over this edge." Chris threatened.

"Yeah do it and see who gets in trouble." James looked at Chris and gave him an evil smile.

Both boys loved the summer. They both loved to go swimming and jump off the cliff by their house. It was easy for them to just slip away whenever mom was working or drunk. Chris and James were as close as any two brothers could be. Growing up all they had was each other.

"James, why don't you just think about what grandma said."

"What? You mean me growing up like grandpa? Having to struggle for everything? No thanks."

"Well then what the hell are you going to do James? Turn out to be like dad, and get shot and killed?"

"At least dad had money." James exclaimed.

"Yeah blood money!"

"You don't know that."

"Oh ok. Keep telling yourself that. Dad died because he got involved with crazy people."

"Chris, dad died because he was stupid and made a bad choice."

"Yeah by getting hooked up with the mob. And when they questioned them, they shut him up. That's what happened to dad. Very stupid choice."

"Look Chris, I'm not dad. I'm not that stupid. I'm not going to get involved with the mob. But I'll be damned if I'm going to be a work class stiff all my life and have to worry about money."

"James I don't want to have to worry about you like I did dad and now mom. You see what dad's death did to mom. All she does now is work and drink. Don't you worry about a family? Don't you want kids some time?"

"Family? Kids? Like we grew up? No thanks. I love you. I always will, you're my brother but like I said I am not going to worry about shit."

"I don't want to see you wind up like dad."

"I know. And I won't. I'm not stupid. I have learned from dad's mistakes."

"Have you?"

"Yes."

"I hope so James, I really do."

They kept swimming at the lake for as long as they could see. But soon, it got so dark that they couldn't tell where the sky and the water met. Neither boy wanted to admit that the other one was right. Neither one wanted to admit that they were secretly afraid of life and how it was going to turn out for the each of them.

Chris didn't remember the year, but he was thinking it was the last time neither one of them were really happy. The last time he remembered having fun with his brother. But that was a lifetime ago. Soon after that they went their separate ways and never spoke to each other again, until recently.

He had been following James for a long time and watching what the hell he was doing. He knew that James had fallen in with wrong crowd and it didn't take much for Mufintano to get his claws in him. But he never imagined that James would grow up to be such a sick perverted bastard.

If it wasn't for the fact he had been drinking again, he would have sworn that he was crying. He knew that he had screwed up his own life, but not to the point of hurting others. Or so he thought. He never had a serious relationship in his entire life. Never had anybody he could talk to when he felt bad. So how different was he from his wayward brother?

The only thing he could ever count on was his time he served in the military at an early age. That was something that he had always been proud of. The Marines had trained him well when it came to learning how to survive and shoot. So well that at some point Chris had been recruited by the CIA and continued to take orders without question.

He often wondered about his life and the choices he made, but he secretly wished he could have saved his brother. James was making terrible choices but he wouldn't listen so Chris finally gave up. It wasn't until Chris was in the Marines that he decided that he could only trust himself, and he knew there would probably never be anyone he would feel close to again.

He was wrong. There was only one person he was remotely close to and he met him in the Marines. They were on a training mission when one of the soldiers miscalculated and a mortar exploded a few mere inches from his new found friend. If it wasn't for the fact that Chris was paying attention, his buddies would have been blown to a million pieces. When you share a close space and a brush with death comes, that tends to make you closer.

Trust came very hard for Chris, even with women. In his mind, it was easier for him to steer clear of any emotional attachments. Sure he had been with plenty of women but there was never any one special person that got to his heart, until now.

Trista got to him wholly. He couldn't explain it but he knew that the minute he seen her when he walked in to Chuggie's. He wanted her in his life. And as soon as he thought of her again, he remembered why he had removed himself from the dating scene. It was for their own good, their own safety.

Part of him wanted to go back and apologize to Trista for what was going to happen to her. But he also knew that she would think he was crazy and probably never want to see him again and that bothered him more. The only thing that he could do was try to watch over her.

Arriving home, he had a million thoughts run throw his mind, like wanting to just once settle down in bed without having to think about who he would wake up with or if he would even wake up at all.

Chapter 41

For as long as Brandie could remember she had been friends with Cassie and now she was in serious trouble. Something was wrong and Brandie had to do something about it. Her town was out of control and somebody needed to protect their own, or there wouldn't be much left.

Brandie was looking forward to going camping and taking Cassie out of this God forsaken town. But where were her parents? They knew she needed to go to the store for a few things for the trip. She wanted to make sure her and Cassie had everything they needed for a week.

Then Brandie realized that she had better call Sheriff Garcia to make sure that it was still ok for Cassie to go with her family. Getting up from her bed to make the call, Brandie thought she heard a noise at the front door. As she walked down the long hall, she remembered her bedroom light on, turning around she stopped in mid-step, and then as quickly as she stopped, she pushed the thought out of her mind and began walking again. It was late, nobody was home and her mind was definitely playing tricks on her. She felt safe simply because Yeager was dead and there wasn't anybody else around that could hurt her or her family. Or so she thought.

Once she walked through the kitchen the phone rang and scared the living hell right out her. After she regained her breathing, she answered the phone, "Hello?"

"Honey are you ok? You seem a little scared."

"Well yeah. I just thought I heard something or somebody at the door and when I got up to go see what it was the phone rang. Bad timing

I guess. Anyway, I should be asking you guys the questions. Where have you been? I tried calling you but nobody was answering the phone."

"We're sorry but we got caught up at your dad's conference and it was taking a little longer than neither one of us expected. We are on our way. We should be there in about an hour."

"Ok mom."

"Are you sure that you're ok?"

"Yeah I'm ok. But I think that maybe you should call Sheriff Garcia just to be safe."

"Ok I will. Just keep the doors locked until we get there."

"See ya in a little bit. I love you mom."

"We love you too." Terri said.

"Bye." They each hung up, Brandie was scared and Terri was telling Jamie to drive faster.

Brandie walked around the whole house. First checking her parents' bedroom since it was the closest to the door, and then she checked the windows, even though they had been locked because it was close to winter. She felt silly about feeling so scared especially since there was a patrol unit outside 24/7 watching the family. It didn't seem to make it any easier, if the bad guys wanted her, they would find a way to get her.

After her nervous of checking windows and doors, Brandie decided to go to bed after one last look out the window to make sure that the unit was still there. Satisfied, Brandie headed back to bed, shutting out all the lights as she walked to her room and locked the door. By sheer coincidence the phone rang when it did, otherwise the house would have been a lot emptier.

"Sonovabitch! Damn phones. Whoever fucking invented them should be shot. We could have had her if weren't the sonovabitch caller. Make sure somebody is here at all times. I want her, if we can't have Cassie! One way or another Garcia well do what we say or more people will wind up like the three dead agents."

"Hey boss? What do you want me to do? I mean it's getting cold."

"Is all you do is fucking whine? Damn just sit there until I tell you not to. *Capiche?*"

They sat there waiting to see what Brandie was going to do next. They couldn't hear the conversation but by the looks of her body language, they knew that Brandie was scared. Whoever called her saved her life, just barely.

"We will take care of her and her family even if it takes the rest of my life. We will take care of her like we took care of Gaston, and we're going to take of her sister too."

"How do you know that there are sisters?"

"Because Gaston raped both women like he violated my Theresa. I'm not fucking stupid, I know that he is the one that took from me and those other women. Why do you think that he moved in across the street? That rat bastard will pay for what he did."

"Look she went to bed. What do you want to do now?"

"We watch her. Her mom and dad have to be coming home soon. And I'm willing to bet that Garcia is going to be somewhere around the corner. We wait. We have to get her alone, totally alone."

"But how long do you want to sit here and wait? I'm getting hungry."

"Are you stupid? Just shut up. If it wasn't for the fact that you were my Cecilia's brother, I would have killed you a long time ago. Holy shit."

"Sorry boss."

For what seemed like forever, both men just sat there with their weapons ready, but it didn't take long before one of them jumped the line.

"I think she went to bed. All of the lights just went out."

"No shit. You think?"

"I'm just saying, what are the chances that she would be staying up all night. We don't even know when her parents are going to be home."

Your sister was right, he mumbled to himself. Both men decided to call it a night the minute they seen Garcia drive up and stop in front of the trailer. He knew that her parents must have called the sheriff when she told them that she heard a noise.

They weren't paranoid about the cruiser, but knew if they didn't leave right away there might be problems, and they didn't want to run the risk of getting caught. It didn't take long for them to leave. Mufintano knew better than to push his luck tonight because one of two things was going to happen. Either they stay and run the risk of the cops finding them or the cops would find another dead body in the bushes because Mufintano was going to kill Cecilia's brother. And neither one the choices was one that he wanted to have to deal with.

Getting back into their car Mufintano kept going over how he wanted to deal with everything. It was a matter time before somebody would find him and try to stop him. He knew that he would do whatever it took so nobody would take him, even if that meant suicide by cop.

Chapter 42

With so many thoughts running through Chris's mind he wasn't sure how he was going to tell Trista who he really was and that her life might be in danger. He couldn't explain his feelings, considering it was just, a mere few hours he had spent with her. He felt like she was the one he wanted to spend the rest of his life with. There was something about Trista that made him feel like he could conquer the world. She made him want to be a better man.

It had been two days since he met Trista but he couldn't get her off his mind. He felt like a kid again when he thought about being with her again. But he also knew if he did choose to stay with her she would surely die. The need to protect and keep her safe was stronger than his need to be with her always.

Chris didn't want to call but he knew he had to call, if it meant never talking to her again. "Is Trista there?" he asked when he called Chuggie's.

"This is Trista. Is there anything I can do for you hun?"

"Trista, this is Chris. I was wondering if we could meet somewhere, I need to talk to you."

"Is everything ok? You seem a little distracted."

"Baby when do you get off work?"

"I'm done in an hour. Where do you want to meet me?" Trista said with a smile that could be felt across the phone line even though it couldn't be seen.

"Nice. Like I said we need to talk. Where can we meet?"

"Ok. Honey you're scaring me. Meet me here in the parking lot and then we can go for a ride and talk. Fair enough?"

"That works. What time?"

"4pm."

"I'll be there waiting. Trista? Be careful."

With that last comment Chris hung up, leaving Trista wondering what the hell was going on. The thought of anybody hurting Trista enraged Chris to a level of no return. He had to warn her somehow even if she didn't believe him, even if she never wanted to see him again, ever.

Pulling into the parking lot at Chuggie's, Chris still wasn't sure what he was going to say to Trista. He wasn't sure what was bothering him the most; having to tell her about the mess his life was in, something he could die from or feeling the way he was feeling. He wasn't sure if it was love or just the fact that he hadn't gotten a piece in a really long time. But either way he knew that he felt compelled to tell her the truth and let fate take over.

No matter what demons he was battling inside him, he couldn't help the smile that crept from ear to ear when he seen Trista walk out the front door. For just a second, everything in Chris's life was alright. He knew that he had to do something.

"Hi baby. How was work?"

"Are you ok Chris? You look like you've seen a ghost."

"Honey, get in. Then I will explain everything."

Trista looked at Chris with a very concerned, very confused look on her face, but she never questioned him. She just got in and put her seat belt on. Once she was settled, Chris started the car back up and took off.

For the longest time nobody spoke. Chris just stared straight ahead, firmly gripping the steering wheel with his left hand and holding Trista's hand with his right. She could tell that something was wrong just by the way he was being silent. Even though she was feeling scared, Trista didn't do or say anything until Chris was ready. For some strange reason she cared for him more than he knew. He didn't know it yet but she would kill for him.

"Trista....."

"Chris. It's ok. Whatever it is, you can tell me."

"God I wish it was that easy."

"What are you talking about? I'm right here. I'm not going anywhere. I promise."

"Trista. I just want you to know that whatever happens, I did not do this on purpose." Chris said as he kissed her gently on the back of her hand.

"What didn't you do on purpose?"

"Trista. I am not who you think I am. See, a long time ago I was in the military, Special Forces. One thing led to another and before I knew it I was deep undercover in with some not nice people. And cliff-notes version, they want me dead and now that I have you, well kind of; your life is in danger. I am afraid that if I stay near you any longer you could wind up like my brother. It still could happen even if I leave you alone. I am so sorry that I ever met you at the bar."

Trista just sat there trying to form her words. Trying to figure out what her next words should be. Then without warning she spoke, from her heart.

"Are you truly sorry that you came in for a drink?"

"Yes I am."

"You could have said no when I asked you to dance. You could have chosen to be an ass and not speak to me at all. But part of you wanted to stay. It doesn't matter what you should or should have not done. It's done. And I am here, now. And I have no regrets. I am glad you came in to my bar. You are exactly what I have been waiting for; a man who is just as conflicted as I am. You should never apologize for past choices you have made. There is a reason for everything. There is a reason why we are here together, now. I have to believe that.

Chris did not know what to say. After hearing Trista talk he was at a loss for words. He never expected to hear that from someone he just met someone like Trista, who would stand by him especially in a situation like this. Before he knew it three hard words came out of his mouth like a bullet.

"I love you......." Chris shocked even himself by saying that.

"Good. Just remember that you said it first. I love you too." Trista said with a coy smile.

"Just one question, why? Why me? You just met me. You don't know me."

"That was actually two questions and to answer the *questions*, because I can feel your heart. I know that you're a good man even though you doubt yourself. So what, you made bad choices. Doesn't everybody at some point in their life? Look, Chris, you can't run scared all of your life. I will be here when this is over." She winked, kissed his hand and readjusted her seatbelt. "So what's next?"

After that conversation, Chris's heart melted, completely. He never thought that he could be so lucky, can't believe how fast this is happening. But his heart is telling him otherwise. He wants Trista in his life, always.

"Well next we need to figure out where you will stay until this over."

"Well don't expect me to quit. That's not going to happen. I will not go running scared.

Who is this mad man anyway?"

"Anthony Mufintano."

"Hmm. Well guess I will have to figure something out. Mufintano's here? In North Muskegon? Wow. And to think I thought that midget wrestling was the most excitement we would ever see around here."

Chris laughed loud and kissed Trista hard. "Is there anything that does scare you?"

"Yes, the thought of losing you."

Both of them did nothing but hold each other like they would never see each other again. They were the perfect match. They both knew one could give the other what they needed. It was a match that could only be taken apart by God. The stars knew what was planned for both of them the night he walked into her bar.

"If you won't stop working here then we need to figure out something else. I will not let him touch you if I can help it." Just then his cell phone rang.

"Yeah."

"You have no clue what you're doing Chris. She will not be safe."

"Who is this?"

"I already told the boss what you were doing. I already told him that you were stalling. And I already told him you have a really cute girlfriend. The boss loved that idea. He figured since your brother took his wife and daughter that it would be a perfect trade. A life for a life."

"Fuck you. You will not touch her. I will see you and him in hell."

"You think so? Let's see if you can get to her before I open that door."

"You sonovabitch, where are you?!"

"Obviously closer than you think brotha."

Without thinking, Chris flung his cell phone in to the back seat pushed Trista down and slammed the door lock just in time to miss the hail of gunfire going through the passenger window.

All of a sudden without Chris seeing it, a red dot appeared on his chest. Out of nowhere a shot rang out from inside the car and then as soon as the gunfire started, it stopped.

"Are you ok? Chris? Are you ok?"

"Yes I'm fine. Are you ok?"

"I told you before. I can take care of myself. I'm fine. I had to shoot him. I saw that red dot on your chest and I wasn't about to lose you already. I'm sorry." and with that Trista broke down. It didn't take long before Chris was tightly holding her in his arms to settle her. He knew that it had to be extremely scary for her and all he wanted to do was calm her.

It took a while before Chris realized he hadn't taken the shot and a minute to realize what Trista was talking about. She saved his life. She killed that man for him.

"Honey, where did you learn to shoot like that? That was a hell of a shot at a long range."

"Let's just say I grew up with a lot male influence."

"Fair enough. Honey we need to get you somewhere safe so I can end this and when it's over we will get to know each better. I promise."

All she could do was nod her answer into his shoulder. Both of them just sat there holding each other knowing that life was short and they had to enjoy the feeling while they could. Because if they weren't careful it would be snatched from them quicker than they expected.

Chapter 43

"Don't touch me!" Cassie screamed. A blinding light came across Cassie's face and then the pain.

"Don't you ever talk to me like that or a member of my crew. You got it?"

"Who are you? Why am I here? What do you want?"

"Don't you worry about it. The only thing you have to worry about is keeping your mouth shut if you want to stay alive. Now just sit still."

"NO! I want to go home. Where is my mom? Where is Sheriff Garcia?" Cassie asked as she kept thrashing about in the chair.

Mufintano didn't like it when someone didn't listen to him. He was the boss and as such should be revered and listened to. He didn't care who she was, he just knew that he was waiting. Waiting, to kill the one man that stood between him and freedom.

"Boss, what do you plan on doing with her?" Frankie asked Mufintano.

"For right now we are keeping her alive. I want to make sure that her daddy shows up."

"You know that the whole sheriff's department, FBI and S.W.A.T everybody will show up? I mean what the hell are you trying to prove?"

"Are you trying to sign your death papers already?" Carlos whispered to Frankie. "No disrespect boss but I am just trying to figure this whole thing out. I mean don't you think that Garcia would have thought about everything? You have that man's daughter. Why wouldn't he have backup?"

"You're not seeing it as usual. Me having Garcia's daughter he will be so outraged that he won't be thinking straight. He will be thinking about just one thing, his daughter. He won't be thinking about whom and what could save him. And if you ever question me again, I will show you who and what won't save you. *Capiche*?"

"Yes boss."

"Now get the message to Garcia that we have his daughter and that he is to come alone, even though I know he won't listen. Make sure that he knows that she is still alive but won't be for long if he doesn't get here soon. Make sure that Garcia knows that I mean business."

"Yes boss."

Nobody questioned Mufintano, at least nobody did if they didn't want to live long. Frankie felt like he had just gotten a new lease on life. He knew that the boss really must have it bad for the sheriff or else he wouldn't be standing there.

"Frankie, are you really brave or just outright stupid? You are one lucky bastard, you know that? The last time someone questioned the boss, it took us five hours to get the gray matter off the walls. Now do what you were told and go back and get that message to the sheriff. He has to know that we aren't playing."

"Carlos, I don't like the feel of this. I'm telling you that something is off here. He has a one track mind. Gaston is dead and we're the ones looking at the death sentence."

"Gaston killed Theresa and I'm willing to bet that he had Cecilia killed too. How the hell would you feel?"

"Fine but don't say that I didn't warn you."

Frankie reluctantly walked out of the warehouse knowing that one of them wasn't going to make it out alive. He knew that before the day was over, someone was going to be going home in a body bag. Frankie sped off not looking back; all the while thinking that he was going to regret the choices he made in life.

Carlos knew better than to even think twice about questioning Mufintano. But by doing so he had the sneaking suspicion that it was him who was going to wind up dead. He owed Mufintano for saving his life so many years ago but now he wonders if he should have just died.

Driving back towards the sheriff's department, Frankie knew something was off. Why was Garcia just standing outside? He should have been running to the hospital or having the whole weight of the department around him. What or who was he waiting for? Was there somebody really watching? Was he being set up by going back there? His stomach began to curl at the possibility. He also knew that either way, he was going to regret it all.

Pulling in to a parking spot at the sheriff department, Frankie noticed that it looked like a ghost town. Nobody was around. Even across the street at the fire department it looked like somebody forgot to pay their electric bill, no movement at all.

Reluctantly, Frankie stepped out of his car and looked around. The fall winds in Muskegon were perfect. Not too hard with just enough wind to force the beautifully colored leaves up off the concrete. It was eerily quiet. No trafffic. No sirens. And amazingly, no gun shots. Frankie felt the fine hairs on the back of his neck stand up and begin to dance.

"What do you want Frankie?"

"Sheriff, we have your daughter." He said as he tightly grabbed the door knob. Raising his 9mm to shoulder level with a perfect bead on Frankies' head, Sheriff Garcia said,

"She better be alive, or believe me I will kill every single one of you bastards before the nights over."

"You know that won't happen. Mufintano wants you, not your daughter." Frankie said with a killer smirk.

"You think just because you work for that worthless piece of shit that you can scare me? Try again. You will not survive another night if anything happens to her."

"Whatever you say, *sheriff.* Just do as you're told and everything will work out. You don't, well you make the call." Frankie got back in to his car, watching the sheriff the whole time while backing up and leaving.

Sheriff Garcia just stood there watching one of the men who stood between him and the sanity of the whole town. He knows that if he wasn't careful, it could turn all wrong. Returning his piece back to its holster, he picked up his phone.

"Frankie Cicero just left here, telling me that they have my daughter. If anything happens to her I will kill him myself. Get everybody in place and here in an hour. Yeah I know, don't worry about it. You just make sure that Brandie is safe. I don't want her nowhere near this place. She was expecting to go camping with Cassie. Yeah I know. She doesn't know anything, and I plan on keeping it that way. Do not tell her anything. You got it? Fine now get here, yesterday."

It was a test of the sheriff's will. Having to do nothing but set there and wait. He knew that with every passing moment, his daughter's life began to shorten. He also knew that the longer he waited, the longer it would be before he could take a piece out of his favorite scumbag.

Pulling up next to the tactical team, Sheriff Garcia got out so he could tell everybody his plan. They were two blocks away from the warehouse where Garcia's daughter was being held and everybody stood around in a circle listening to every word that was being said. Nobody thought twice about leaving and everybody reveled in getting their chance at taking down one of the most feared men in the twentieth century.

"I want everybody to make sure that all points of entry are covered. I don't want any of those bastards to have a chance of getting out, and remember that my daughter is in there right in the middle of that hell. Nobody knows what Mufintano has in store for us. Nobody knows how many people are in there. The only thing we know is that Mufintano and his crew is heavily armed. Now you all have one more chance to walk. If you choose to do so, do it now."

Nobody moved. They all just stood there looking at each other, waiting to hear what Sheriff Garcia's last few words. They all checked to make sure that their shit was in order and waited to hear the last few words that Sheriff Garcia had to say.

"You all better be paying real close attention, because when I drop my gun that will be the signal. Remember my daughter is in there and I want Mufintano and his crew alive, especially Anthony. Do not kill him. Do you all understand?"

They all nodded in unison. They were all anxious to get this whole thing over with. None of them were afraid but cautious because of who they were up against. They all also knew that no matter what the outcome was, they would be either known as really brave or really stupid.

Chapter 44

"Sheriff, we'll find her. I promise." said Sergeant Harris.

"If Mufintano hurts one hair on Cassie's body I will kill him myself. I don't care who the hell he is or how much fucking power and fear he carries. I will see him in hell if he hurts my daughter."

Sergeant Harris and the rest of the tactical team left to get in to position. Sheriff Garcia was no longer thinking like a lawman, his thinking was clouded by the fact that his daughter had been taken. But Sheriff Garcia didn't care if he was running the risk of dying or not. All that mattered to him was making sure that his daughter would make it out alive. He knew about Mufintano's reputation, he knew what Mufintano did to his victims and if Cassie became his latest victim, she would never be found again.

Carefully pulling up towards the rear of warehouse, Garcia checked in with the other members of the tactical team, making sure that they were in position. Sgt Harris was the first to check in followed by the rest of them. Sheriff Garcia knew that he only had one chance at rescuing his newly found life.

With everybody in place, the S.W.A.T team was ready to rush in and the sharp shooters on the roofs of the surrounding buildings, it was time. Sheriff Garcia told everybody "On my count, then I want everybody to rush in but be careful, my daughter is in there with Mufintano and I'll be damned she will wind up collateral damage. Everybody watch their asses, he's heavily armed so is every member of his crew."

The S.W.A.T team members broke down the wall and everybody else swarmed the building from every point of entry possible. It was dark inside. All the windows were covered with what seemed like black felt paper, they could barely see save for the beams of sunlight breaking through the boards above.

"Let her go Anthony and we can all walk out of here alive."

"I can't do that Garcia, you know what it's like, not trusting anyone. Plus what does it matter if I off her or not? You guys are trying to fucking blame me for her step fathers murder. Why the fuck would I give up the only leverage I've got?" Mufintano said as he positioned himself behind Cassie.

"Anthony, we can talk about this." Sheriff Garcia said he continued to watch his daughter while the rest of tactical team formed a circle around Mufintano and his crew. Everybody had their guns drawn and trained on somebody, ready to shoot and Cassie sat on a chair in the middle. All she could do was cry and pray that she didn't get caught in the crossfire.

"Yeah right. What is she to you? How much of your life are you willing to sacrifice to make sure that your little girl gets out of here? You move any closer I swear to God I'll shoot her. I might not get out of here alive but I will make sure that I take some of you bastards with me. Now back the fuck up." Tensions were high and nobody thought about moving.

"Why Anthony? Why the hell did you go through such great lengths to erase James Gaston? That doesn't make any sense. There was no proof that he killed Theresa. Do you really want to go out like this? You might get off the shot that kills me or my daughter but I guarantee that none of you will get out of here alive. Do you really want to die?"

"Sheriff, you have no clue what I care about. So don't fucking try to act like you're my friend. Back the fuck up or she dies." Mufintano said as he pushed the muzzle of the Beretta harder to the back of her head. But what he didn't know was that Cassie was already out from the severe beating she took when Mufintano first got her to the warehouse.

Sheriff Garcia had already talked to the sharp shooters, telling them that when they have a clear shot, to shoot. But he told them not to kill, he told them to take a shoulder or leg shot that he wanted Mufintano alive, the same with the rest of the crew.

"Ok, Anthony. Look I am putting my gun down. Just don't do anything stupid." That was Garcia's signal. Gun shots rang out and in an instant it was blood bath and Anthony Mufintano, Frankie Cicero and another unnamed man lay unmoving on the ground and everybody rushed in.

The FBI, sheriff deputies and members from the swat team all ran to the three men lying on the ground. Quickly they were handcuffed and placed in to separate police cars. The whole time, Mufintano was cursing, swearing that he would beat it, get out and see Sheriff Garcia dead.

Sheriff Garcia scrambled to untie Cassie from the chair and without thinking, picked her up and ran outside to the awaiting police cruiser. He knew that he should wait for an ambulance but this was his daughter, he thought that he could get her to the hospital quicker. The whole drive to the hospital seemed like it took hours.

Right before getting to the hospital, Garcia called Jessica and told her to meet him at the hospital, he found Cassie and that Mufintano was less than gracious to her. He apologized for how everything turned out, he loved her and he would make sure that Cassie would be avenged if anything happened to her. What Jessica heard scared her, but she told Ray she would meet him there.

Cassie lay in her hospital bed hooked up to a bunch of I.Vs and a ventilator, surrounded by both of her parents, her best friend Brandie and Daphne and what seemed like half of the hospital staff; all praying that Cassie would pull through, not knowing if their prayers would be answered.

No one imagined that something like this could happen in their own back yards. North Muskegon had been a place where the worse that happened were kids skipping school. They never thought that one of their own would be lying in a bed at deaths door.

Jessica was the one to finally speak, "What happens now? What is going to happen to the ones that did this to our daughter?"

"I'm not sure honey. I know that the prosecuting attorney is trying to charge Mufintano with a multitude of different charges like kidnapping, attempted murder and assault and battery to say the least. That bastard is really lucky that he didn't violate Cassie, I would kill him where he stood if he did."

"What about the other two men that were working with Mufintano? What happens to them?"

"The shot to Frankie Cicero's chest was fatal, he didn't make it. Carlos and Mufintano will be arraigned and prosecuted."

One by one Brandie, AJ and Daphne all left. There really wasn't anything they could do for Cassie at that point but wait and hope. Both Sheriff Garcia and Jessica told them if anything changed they would call them immediately.

Once alone, Garcia and Jessica just sat there and held each other, not knowing if anything would change. Neither of them was sure if their daughter was strong enough to pull through. Jessica closed her eyes and cried. Ray closed his eyes, but he didn't cry. He wondered about how much security there would be in prison for Mufintano.

Sheriff Garcia was an upstanding member of the community, and the thoughts going through his mind were of rage and revenge and that shocked him. He never once thought about intentionally harming another human being, until now. Ray prayed that somebody would get to Mufintano in prison, because if an inmate didn't get to him, he realized that Anthony Mufintano would for the first time be sitting in the crosshairs of a father scorned.

Chapter 45

One week later

Doctors and nurses buzzed around the third floor ICU without a care in the world. Of course they all cared about their patients but they had so much to do they could only spend so much time with each one.

After Nurse Dennison checked Cassie's blood pressure and other vitals, and checked on her coma status, she went on to her next patient. But as she was getting ready leave her room, Nurse Dennison was met with Sheriff Garcia. He asked her how Cassie was doing; she didn't divulge any pertinent information other than saying that she hadn't had a change in her condition.

The nurse left the room and Sheriff Garcia stood there at the end of her bed, looking and praying that she would wake up. Hoping that one day he would get the chance to talk to his daughter. Talk to her and explain everything.

Ray took a chair from by the window and sat it next to her bed and sat down. The tears just started to flow, he grabbed her hand and kissed it ever so gently, then lay his forehead down on the edge of her bed and kept saying over and over again "I am so sorry honey. I didn't know. I wouldn't have ever left you if I ever suspected this would happen. I know that you probably hate me for not being there for you but please I will make it up to you. I promise."

All he could do was cry. The adrenaline was finally returned back to normal and the bad guys were where they belonged. Mufintano was in a maximum security prison without any chance of parole with the few remaining crew, which were left after the major shoot out in the warehouse. Jessica finally agreed to married Chewy. Agent Kovac went back to Quantico to brief her superiors on the whole investigation and Agent Ritter recuperated and stayed behind to finish dealing with the local police.

The wedding was marvelous; as sunny and beautiful as any great summer day could be in Hawaii. Jessica was dressed in all white strapless dress with a train that went on for at least ten feet. Cassie was wearing a hunter green, floor length, flowing spaghetti strap dress that accented her red hair and blue eyes. And Brandie was wearing a midnight blue dress that looked identical to Cassie's.

Both Ray and Jessica prepared their own vows. The ceremony was a tear jerker, with not a dry eye in house. They said their respective I do's and then Father Tom presented the new couple to audience. But just as Ray and Jessica had turned around to look at everybody that was present, flesh and blood shot out of Jessica's chest.

A look of sheer terror came over Ray's face and then she collapsed. Before Jessica died, she whispered two things to Ray 'She really is your daughter. I will always love you.' and then she was gone. Garcia scrambled for his gun but he couldn't find it. He checked both hips, his pockets, hell he even checked his boots, nothing.

Ray looked up to see a man come running at him and his newly dead bride. But for some reason he couldn't see the shooters face, it was obscured by a blinding light. The next thing he knew he felt a searing pain shooting through his shoulder.

"You?! But how could you, I thought that you were..."

"You're right. For you I was dead. What do you think that you could forget about me? Leave me for dead in that fucking swamp and pray that nobody would ever find me? You deserted me. You left me for dead. And now I am just supposed go about my fucking life like nothing has changed? You will pay for the pain that you caused me. You will pay for all of those years that I was alone. You no good bastard, I want you to witness the pain as Jessica slowly dies. I want you to see pain, so you know what it feels like before you die too."

"But how? I didn't know that you were alive. You have to believe. I didn't know."

"Bullshit!! You knew and did nothing. And now you must pay for your sins."

With that last painful comment, Ray took one last breath before HE raised his hand to shoulder level and pulled the trigger. The sound of the shot echoed in Ray's head as the bullet traveled towards his head in what seemed like forever. And right before the bullet entered Ray's brain, he heard a quiet girl's voice. "Daddy? Daddy, why are you just.................."

A loud bang woke Ray out of his reverie. Feeling his shoulders and his head, for a split second he didn't realize that it was just a dream. His rapid breathing finally slowed. Perspiration still present on his face, Ray looked around to see if anybody else was in the room.

"What the hell kind of dream was that?' He thought to himself. Even though he knew it was just a dream, it still bothered him. He knew that the guilt was going to follow him for a long time. The only thing he could pray for was that someday he would come to terms with it all.

Laying his head back down on the edge of Cassie's hospital bed, something stopped him in his tracks. What was it? He couldn't be sure. Then he heard it again. Then slowly he turned his head towards Cassie. And there she was, looking right at him with a smile on her face. "Daddy."

The only thing that Sheriff Garcia could do was smile, hold her hand and cry. "Hi baby, how are you feeling?"

"What happened?"

"Shhh. Don't worry about what happened. I am just so glad that you are ok. Look, we have a lot of time to make up for and hell I'm not even sure where to start, but I want you to know that I love you and I will always be here for you."

"You don't have to try and explain anything to me. I know that you didn't know about me. Mom explained it all to me right before this. Maybe one day we can talk and you could come and visit sometimes."

"I would love that. But I want you to know, I want to be around as much as you will let me, when you are ready, I want to be a dad to you. I want to be in your life. And for what it's worth, I am truly sorry."

"I know daddy. It's ok. Some things are out of your control. Sometimes the choices we make just come back to bite us in the ass. And sometimes we really do get second chances. Not everybody knows how to deal with those second chances. But something tells me that you and I will get along and be just fine."

Ray didn't know what to say. He didn't realize how grown up his little girl really was. All he could do was look at her with the utmost admiration and pride. He wondered how he was going to make up for all of the lost time. How was he ever going to repay her for giving him his life back?

Just about the time he was going to say something to Cassie, the door opened. The one person that neither of them expected to walk through the door with Jessica was right before their eyes.

Special Agent Eric Ritter was standing side by side with Cassie's mom. All Ray could do was stare at his future. From the minute he laid eyes on her again, he knew Jessica was the one that he wanted to spend the rest of his life. Without her, he was nothing.

Cassie wasn't looking for anybody when she met Agent Ritter. Her life was already a mess; let alone taking on an emotional rollercoaster of a relationship. But all Eric had to do was just say 'Hi' and Cassie knew there would be no one else for her but him. Cassie fell in love with him from the moment she laid eyes on him.

Eric Ritter was a beautiful man at 5'8", 180 pounds and electric blue eyes. He didn't think he was nothing special, but to her he was everything. He made her want to be a better woman.

"Hi." Eric said. "I'm sorry. I am so sorry that I didn't tell you about me, but I couldn't. I couldn't compromise my position. I love you and I hope that one day, you would come to believe me. I just wanted to stop by and make sure that you are ok. I'm sure somebody will let me know when you get out of the hospital. Take care."

"Don't...go...please....I....love ....you....too."

They all knew that from that moment on that everything was going to be just fine. They finally found what they were looking for after a lifetime of hell. They both found that one true love, their forever soul mates. From now on life could only get better. They both found what and who they were looking for; faith, love and happiness.

Epilogue

Six months later............

Kevin and Trista got more comfortable with each other also after the Mufintano mess. Trista forgave Kevin for lying to her about who he was and Trista in turn gave him her heart fully. It wasn't long before they moved in together and started living their lives in peace. Trista finally, one night, told Kevin the reason why she was able to shoot so good. It was because she was a newbie Marine and very well trained. So well trained that she was able to save a group of men that were held up and taking fire. She took the shots at a thousand plus yards. The only thing she regretted was that she never got to meet the members of the fire-team.

Trista went back to work at Chuggie's and each night went home to the one person who made her feel safe and whole. Kevin never imagined in his whole miserable life he would find someone who he could be himself around or want to love unconditionally. Together they were a match.

Sheriff Garcia and Jessica finally got the one thing that they both wanted, to be joined together forever. After what seemed like eternity, the wedding went off without a hitch with both of them totally focused on each other. Their love, their bond, was unquestionable. It was a love that any normal person could only hope for on their very best day.

AJ and Butch enjoyed each other as much as they could considering Butch had confessed and was arrested for killing Robert Yeager a.k.a. James Gaston. AJ would go and see Butch as much as she could if she wasn't in the middle of a case for the FBI. If she wasn't working a case, AJ was a mounting a strategy to help get Butch out of jail.

Daphne finally found someone that could handle her.......from the moment Tobias met Daphne he knew that she would be a handful and that there would never be a dull moment in his life.

Daphne and Tobias went about their lives without a care or anymore problems. Tobias talked to Daphne constantly about her new found siblings, trying to ensure her that everything be ok. Daphne in turn trusted him completely. After their wedding, which was attended by everybody, they couldn't wait to start their new lives together beginning with their honeymoon in Playa Del Carmen Mexico. New love was definitely in the air.

Sometime after the mess with Mufintano, Cassie attempted to get what was left of her life back in order. She eventually got discharged from the hospital with a clean bill of health. Her mom and dad finally got married and have been happy ever since. And Cassie got the one thing that she always wanted, true love.

Agent Eric Ritter unwittingly fell in love with the one person he told himself he wouldn't ever think about, Cassie Damien. During his three month investigation with the Mufintano case he told himself he wouldn't get involved with one of the prime suspects but lo-and-behold he did anyway and Cassie herself was just as receptive.

After their first nervous date, they both began to loosen up. They both called each other incessantly and hated the thought of having to hang up. The age difference didn't bother them. Cassie was just turning 19 and Eric was 26. Both knew early on that they didn't want anybody else in their lives.

Agent Ritter put in for a transfer to be closer to Cassie and she in turn did what she had to do to be more understanding during the transition. It was six months in to their relationship before he asked Cassie to move in with him. It took Cassie a whole thirty seconds to decide what to do. Cassie knew what she wanted and wasn't afraid to go after it. They both realized that life was too short to care what other people thought of them.

"Eric, baby would you please call me sometime tonight? I just need to know that you are ok."

"You know that I will be ok. But yes I will call you when I get the chance. Have you talked to anybody about those nightmares you have been having?"

"Not yet but I will. I just........"

"No buts. You need to talk to someone honey. It's not like you got lost in the woods for a night. You were drugged, abducted, beaten....."

"Do I need to be here for this? I know what happened to me."

"All I am saying is that I love you and I can't stand the fact that you are going through this. I can only imagine what it was like. And even though you lived and Mufintano and his soldiers are either dead or in prison, it is still fresh in your head. Please tell me that you will get some help soon? I will be right here besides you."

"I know you will and I love you for it. I just don't think it's that much of a big deal. It's my brains' way of dealing the stress and shit I have been through."

"I know honey but it has been six months I would think that by now your brain would have processed most of it."

"Ok. I am going to let you go. I have housework to do and you need to get back to work. Be safe. I love you. Good night."

"I love you. I will and good night." Each one hung up and went about their business.

It was some time later when Cassie's phone rang again. "Geez Eric I didn't know that you........."

"Cassie honey its daddy. I need you to meet me at Mercy ER right away."

"Dad, what's going on? I'm waiting for Eric to come home."

"He's not coming home honey. Eric's been shot. They worked on him for over two hours they said. The doctor told me that he may be in a coma indefinitely."

Cassie dropped the phone and collapsed on the floor. She couldn't believe that the man she agreed to marry was in a coma again. There were no details yet, other than it was a drive by shooting. Agent Ritter was getting ready to get in to his car and he took fire. Nobody knows how many more people out there that was beyond evil.

Printed in the United States
By Bookmasters